Hayden

Hayden

BREAKAWAY HOCKEY #1

S.R. GREY

Hayden (Breakaway Hockey #1)
Copyright © 2023 by S.R. Grey

ISBN-13: 979-8-9866072-3-8

Editing: Hot Tree Editing
Proofreading: Deaton Author Services
Beta Readers: Franci N. and JoAnna E.
Cover Photographer: Wander Aguiar Photography
Model: Chase Roback
Cover Design: Najla Qamber
Formatting:

emtippettsbookdesigns.com

Books by
S.R. GREY

Breakaway Hockey series
Hayden

Boys of Winter series
Destiny on Ice
Resistance on Ice
Complications on Ice
Caution on Ice
Player on Ice
Vows on Ice
Illusion on Ice
Forbidden on Ice
Bet on Ice
Dare on Ice
Risk on Ice

Men of Fall series
Forward Progress
Fair Catch
Eligible Receiver
Down by Contact
Hard Count

Judge Me Not series
I Stand Before You
Never Doubt Me
Just Let Me Love You
The After of Us

Inevitability duology
Inevitable Detour
Inevitable Circumstances

Promises series
Tomorrow's Lies
Today's Promises

A Harbour Falls Mystery trilogy
Harbour Falls
Willow Point
Wickingham Way

Laid Bare novella series
Exposed: Laid Bare 1
Unveiled: Laid Bare 2
Spellbound: Laid Bare 3
Sacrifice: Laid Bare 4

Chapter One

HAYDEN

I stretch my legs out in front of me as my fellow passengers file in.

Ahhh, I love first class.

It's especially nice since I'm in the front row with only the bulkhead before me. And—*bonus!*—so far, nobody has taken the window seat to my left.

Yeah, we'll see how long that lasts.

Chuckling, I cross one ankle over my knee and run my hand down my dark-wash jeans. When I lift my gaze, the bubbly blonde flight attendant assigned to first class makes eye contact.

Again.

She's already checked on me twice in the past eight minutes or so.

I smile cordially, and she scampers over.

Reaching me in lightning speed, she gulps in a breath of air and asks, "Would you like a bottle of water, sir? It's nice and cold."

Oh, what the hell.

"Sure," I reply.

As she hands me the indeed icy cold water, she says, "Let me know if there's anything else you need or want. I'm here to make your flight as comfortable as possible, Mr. Harrington."

Ah, so she does know who I am. I suspected as much. This explains the enthusiastic and more-than-necessary fawning over me.

I'm pretty sure this flight crew is from here in Chicago, so it's no real surprise. I've played hockey for the Blackhawks for the past four years.

Speaking of which, I kind of expected to stay longer. But after a big-ass mistake on my part—a fling with the coach's daughter that didn't end well—the writing was on the wall.

Sure enough, I was traded a little over a week ago.

Since we're halfway through September, I'm currently on my way to Georgia to start with the Atlanta Thunder, the team I was traded to.

The Thunder is an expansion team with a decent inaugural season under their belt. They had a very good top line, but their center, an OG veteran who was looking to play a little more hockey before hanging up his skates, decided to retire in May.

That left them with a big-ass opening, one that needs to be filled.

I'm a power forward who can play left wing *or* center. I'm pretty sure that's why the Thunder decided to take a chance on me, even with my bad-boy reputation.

But I can't get too far ahead of myself. I'm not a shoo-in for the top line. I'll need to work for it.

I heard through the hockey grapevine that the Thunder's second-line center, a dude named Finn Norath, will also be vying for the job.

Too bad for him, I intend to earn it.

When I see something I want, I go for it.

Sometimes it lands me in trouble—like with the coach's daughter—but most of the time it works out in my favor.

I think about the coach's daughter now and how it irks me to no end that a damn low-level marketing intern for the Blackhawks busted my ass. If it wasn't for her, no one would have ever known we'd had a fling.

It was over anyway.

So why did that intern divulge my secret?

Why did Addison Knight have it out for me?

I'll never forget her name. Or, to be honest, her stunning good looks. Her long, raven hair, toned hot body, and pretty green eyes would have captivated me under any other circumstances.

I would have wanted to get to know her.

But not now, not ever.

In fact, I never want to cross her path.

Nope. Even though she's hot as sin, I'm beyond thankful that I'll never have to see her or deal with her ever again.

Come to think of it, why am I even thinking about her?

Yeah, stop this nonsense.

Shaking my head to get Addison's annoyingly pretty face out of my thoughts, and then taking a swig of cool water, I erase her from my mind.

With a clear head, I focus on the people who are still boarding. It's been a slow process today, as the trail of passengers seems never-ending.

I can see why—it's like everyone coming onboard has a carry-on that needs to be stowed.

And fuck, now someone is stopping at my row—a man with white hair, wearing a dark navy blue business suit.

He shoves a bag into the compartment above me, then, making eye contact, he clears his throat and says, "Excuse me. I'm in 1A."

As he waves to the window seat, I lower my foot from my leg and reply, "Sure, no problem."

As he slips by me and takes his seat, I sigh quietly.

So much for having the row all to myself.

Oh, well.

I'm just happy this is first class and there's a console between us. It gives us both some extra arm space.

Good thing, too, as he just opened his newspaper and fluffed it out.

That's okay. I take it this means he's not going to want to talk.

Relieved, I blow out a breath.

Twisting to peer back at the rows behind me, I notice there's only one empty seat remaining in first class. It's in the last row on the opposite side.

Interesting, as the plane appears to be otherwise full.

There's no one boarding anymore.

I guess someone is just running late.

Just as I'm turning back around to face forward, I hear a woman I can't yet see, as she's behind the bulkhead, apologizing to the blonde flight attendant who gave me the water.

I catch her final heartfelt-sounding "I'm so sorry."

And then she steps into view.

Holy crap!

I'm stunned.

I'm speechless.

I'm somewhat horrified.

No, I'm definitely fully horrified.

The woman notices me staring as she starts down the aisle. And then her big emerald eyes widen.

Oh, she knows who I am—the man whose reputation she ruined—just like I know who she is.

Okay, to be fair, I did a lot of that reputation-ruining on my own with my behavior. Still, it was her blabbing about my ill-advised fling that sealed the deal with the Blackhawks.

Like my nemesis can't help herself, she comes to a faltering halt by my row.

I look up at her.

And then I'm kind of gawking.

Why?

Well, for a beat, though it's crazy, I think she's checking me out.

But that can't be right.

I shake my head, and she narrows her eyes at me.

Now she just looks irritated.

This is unbelievable. I never thought I'd see her ever again. And why, when I do, does she have to be wearing a sexy, formfitting black dress that accentuates her every perfect curve?

I don't know, but I'm unabashedly checking her out.

Take that, sweetheart.

If we were strangers, I'd try to get to know her, maybe even ask her out.

Hey, she's heading to Atlanta, too, right?

But none of that will ever happen...because of who she is.

I'd never ask her out—not here, not now, not if my life depended on it.

Yeah, this woman, who just rolled her emerald eyes at me before she huffed and took off down the aisle, is fucking Addison Knight—my nemesis, my enemy, the one who ratted me out, the one who ran me out of Chicago.

Disgusted, I roll my own damn eyes.

I can't get to Atlanta fast enough.

I just want to get the hell away from her, this time forever.

Chapter

Two

ADDISON

What the ever-loving hell?

How is this happening?

How am I on the same flight as Hayden Harrington?

Ugh!

I knew the jerk was traded to Atlanta, but what's the chance we'd be leaving Chicago at the same time?

Flustered, I stop in my tracks. Just to stare at the asshole and make him uneasy.

It seems to work, as his icy blue eyes meet mine.

Why do they have to be so striking?

Why must he be so hot and sexy in general?

I can't help it. My traitorous eyes move over his muscular quads, defined even under the dark denim fabric of his jeans. And then I'm taking in his broad shoulders and wide chest.

Mmm, he's looking good in that pale blue polo shirt.

Oooh, and his mussed-up chestnut-brown hair looks like it needs someone to run their fingers through it.

Maybe it should be me?

No, wait, what am I thinking?

Never would I do such a thing, not in this lifetime.

His fine attributes, that some lunatic part of me likes, angers me further.

I narrow my eyes at him.

See, I hate you, dude.

Huffing, I hustle my ass to my row in the back of first class.

Thank God I'm not seated next to Hayden, I think as I stow my carry-on in the compartment above me.

With one more huff, I settle my butt into the aisle seat.

But my mind is still on the man I love to hate.

Hayden Harrington drives me nuts.

There, I said it.

Not only did he mess around with the coach's daughter, Kristi—a friend of mine who is tall and thin and always wears her long blonde hair in a high ponytail—but he freaking broke her heart.

Worse yet, I don't think the jackass even realized it.

Although, in his defense, she never let him know she was all that upset.

Wait, why am I defending him?

He should have realized something was up.

The girl just looked so sad.

How clueless could he be?

I guess a lot clueless since he actively avoided her once it was all over, as quickly as it had begun.

What a cad.

What a cocky ass.

She told me once that he was a player, as in a ladies' man.

It was supposedly in the past, but he clearly hadn't changed.

So I told on him.

I did it mainly as a favor for Kristi. She wanted her dad to know so he'd be hard on Hayden during practices.

But it went too far.

Harrington got traded.

I cringe.

Yeah, as much as I hated what he'd done, I didn't expect that. I think even Kristi was shocked.

I'm still conflicted about the way it went down. I was kind of the "bad guy" in the situation.

But so was he.

Ugh, so much confusion.

All I know is I can't stand the man.

Because of that, I was kind of relieved when I heard he'd been traded to the Atlanta Thunder.

I figured I wouldn't have to see or think about him ever again.

But then, just a few days ago, I landed a job with the same team.

Talk about crazy.

Once my internship with the Chicago Blackhawks ended—with many accolades and a slew of recommendations—I interviewed with a lot of teams across the league. I had my pick in most cases, but my best offer came from the Thunder.

I had to accept the position with them. I'd have been remiss not to.

So I did, and now I'm joining their marketing and public relations department on Monday. My job is with the player image development team. I'll be what they call a "consultant."

It should be a cool job.

I hope to eventually have a chance to give my input on events and hopefully even organize a few on my own. But the most fun will be in working directly with the guys on promoting positive, fun things, as well as highlighting all the good they do in the community.

I think about how I'll most likely never have to work with Hayden Harrington.

Nope, that dude never did any promo stuff in Chicago.

I suspect his time in Atlanta will be the same.

But you never know.

At that thought, a chill runs down my spine.

I sure hope Hayden doesn't change his ways, as the thought of working with him makes me ill.

Peeking out from under my lashes, I sneak a glance up at the man I love to hate.

But I can only see his right shoulder.

Quickly, I look back down.

Phew.

I'm glad he didn't turn around and catch me.

So I'm not tempted to try that dumb move again, I close my eyes.

And then I think about how this flight can't end soon enough.

Chapter

Three

HAYDEN

A h, *Monday morning, and I'm here at my first practice with the* Thunder.

It's still training camp, though, as the regular season doesn't start for one more week.

I missed the first few days, since the trade hadn't officially gone through immediately, but it doesn't seem to matter one little bit.

This practice couldn't be going any better than if I had scripted it.

Coach Barnes, a middle-aged ex-defenseman who's known for having great chemistry with his players, originally had me at center on the second line. Finn, no surprise, was up on the first.

But nothing was going right.

Now Coach has *me* on the top line at the center position, teamed up with Arden Troy at left wing and Nils Sten on my right.

We're in the last few minutes of what's been a lively scrimmage between Squad B, my "team," and Squad A.

We're currently up 3-2.

I haven't scored a goal yet, but I assisted on two.

The first one, Arden picked up a pass from me before burying the puck deep in the net. Nils also got a goal in a neat tic-tac-toe play I quarterbacked a few minutes ago.

We're on the bench at the moment, catching our breath, but not for long.

As soon as the second line comes off the ice, we jump on.

That's when I notice a defenseman on Squad A is losing control of the puck right at center ice.

I pounce on it, and since no one else is around, I go on a breakaway.

Yes!

I skate up the ice as quickly as I can, which is faster than my pursuers.

And then it's just me and the goalie.

I fake him out by pretending to shoot low in the corner.

When he goes down, I lift the puck up and over his shoulder.

Gotcha!

My fake-out is a success, and I score the goal unassisted.

Time runs out, and we win 4-2.

Afterward, in the locker room, the mood is amazing. Even my teammates who were on the opposing squad give me props.

Finn, the second-line center, taps me on the shoulder as he walks by. "Nice goal, Harrington," he says. "Keep it up."

I nod in humble acknowledgment. "Thanks, man."

Arden, standing on my right, pulls his practice jersey up over his head. He then discards his black tech undershirt.

Bare-chested and with his jet-black hair sticking up in all kinds of crazy angles, he sits down on the bench next to me and says, "You looked really solid out there, Hayden."

"Yeah," Nils, seated on the other side of me, chimes in. "If the rest of training camp goes this well with the three of us paired up, I think we know where you'll be starting the first game of the season."

Yeah, top line at center, just as I planned.

I don't articulate that out loud.

Instead, blowing out a breath, I say, "I sure hope so. We do have good chemistry, that's for sure. It's like we've been playing together for a while."

"For sure," the guys agree.

Arden then asks me if I'd like to go to lunch with them after we're showered and dressed.

I'm all in, as getting to know these guys can only serve to make us a stronger unit on the ice.

But it's not just that. There's a bigger reason than simple hockey goals.

The truth is I could use a couple friends. I was too much of a loner in Chicago, and look how that turned out.

I guess I'm turning over a new leaf.

I just want my time in Atlanta to be different…in a lot of ways.

An hour or so later, Arden, Nils, and I are seated on the back patio of a casual restaurant. It's good that the vibe is laid-back since we're all in jeans and tees.

Lunch has gone great so far.

I'm glad I accepted the invitation to join these two. The big steak salads we're eating are tasty, and conversation is flowing nicely. It's been mostly all hockey talk, rehashing our awesome scrimmage and discussing plays.

I like these guys.

They're cool.

Arden is definitely the more outgoing of the two. Don't get me wrong. Nils is personable and all, but more chill.

In any case, I feel like all three of us are getting along beautifully. I hope we stay paired up on the top line.

A small breeze kicks up, and a strand of Nils's longish blond hair blows across his cheek.

Brushing it away, he leans back in his chair and asks, "So, Hayden, where are you staying for now? Did the team put you up in one of those extended-stay hotels? I know that's fairly standard procedure."

I shake my head. "Actually, no, I'm not in a hotel." I take a small bite of steak from my salad, and then lower my fork. After I swallow, I say, "When my agent told me the Thunder were interested in me, I got online and checked out some house rentals. There was one I really liked, fully furnished, and not too big or too small. Anyway, I put a deposit down on it the minute the trade went through. So, yeah, that's where I'm at for at least the next six months. If things go well here, I'll look into buying something then."

"Sounds like a plan." Nils nods approvingly. "Where's this house located?"

"Up in Woodstock," I reply.

"I'm not far from there."

Jumping into the conversation, Arden says, "Yeah, you're both in a good location. You don't have too far of a drive to get to the arena. I bought property way up north and had a house built on a big-ass piece of wooded land. I love being out in the middle of nowhere, but the commute sucks sometimes. Still, all things considered, I wouldn't change a thing."

I reply truthfully, "I don't mind driving. I think I'd prefer something more secluded as well. But that's a thought for down the road."

"Yeah." Arden nods. "Just concentrate on the present for now. You have enough new crap going on."

I can't argue with that.

The boys ask me a few more questions about the rental, so I share that it's in a quiet neighborhood, tucked away on a secluded cul-de-sac with only one other house.

"Nice," Arden says. "That sounds really private."

"That's what I'm hoping for," I reply. Then, thinking back to when I first came across the listing, I add, "One crazy thing was that the other house, the one next to mine, was for rent also. I looked into that one, and it has almost the exact same layout on the inside, just switched up, like a mirror image. Oh, and the exterior of the other one is stone. Mine is brick. I like that look better. Plus"—I chuckle—"the house I chose is slightly bigger."

"Hey, bigger is always better," Nils replies, laughing.

Arden, finished with his salad, pushes his plate away. Wiping his mouth with a napkin, he says, "Well, if they do rent the other house, let's hope you end up with a good neighbor, seeing as it's so close to yours."

"Hell." I raise my water glass. "I'll drink to that."

Chapter

Four

ADDISON

I spend the whole weekend settling into my new home. It's just a rental, though, so I won't be here forever.

Still, it's perfect for now—a beautiful stone structure located on a little cul-de-sac in the very back of a quiet plan.

The best part is I have only one neighbor—a neighbor I have yet to see or meet.

All I've noticed so far is there's often a dark blue SUV parked in the driveway out front. I saw it there this morning after I woke up.

I think it's a rental. It has an out-of-state North Carolina license plate on it, just like how my beige sedan from Enterprise has a Florida tag.

I'm having my own car—an older white BMW—driven down from Chicago. It should be here next week, along with a bunch of my clothes and personal belongings I loaded into it before I left.

Speaking of which, I can't wait to have the rest of my things arrive at the house. I didn't pack a lot in the suitcase I brought on Friday, and I found myself hard-pressed this morning choosing an outfit for my first day.

Luckily, I do have two pantsuits—one black, one gray—and some nice blouses to wear under the matching jackets.

I can also utilize the dress I flew down in. It's a little tight and short for business, but if I pair it with one of the jackets, I should be good.

Maybe I'll wear the dress tomorrow, I think as I leave the house and hit the road for my first day on the job.

The drive down to the arena, where the Thunder's corporate offices are located, is pretty darn quick.

I park in the employee lot, and, taking a deep breath and exhaling slowly in order to calm my nerves, I hop out of my rental car and head in.

The day goes really well.

Most of the morning is spent completing new hire paperwork and attending orientation sessions.

After a quick lunch in my little office, I meet all of my fellow team members. They seem really nice and cordial. We discuss some of the upcoming events and go over new ideas for future ones.

Finally, at the end of the day, I'm exhausted but feel amazing.

Before I leave, I have one final meeting with my boss, Ms. Garcia.

Her secretary, Miss Horne, sends me into a spacious office, where I'm directed to take a seat opposite a large dark wood desk.

"Ms. Garcia will be with you in a minute," Miss Horne informs me.

"Thank you," I reply.

She leaves, closing the door behind her, and I tuck a wayward strand of hair behind my ear.

I'm a little nervous and have to resist the urge to fidget. Even though Ms. Garcia is the person who hired me, this is my first time meeting her face-to-face. I'm also curious as to what this meeting may entail.

I guess I'll find out what I'll be doing tomorrow, since today was all introductory stuff.

I hope I'll be working with a player, and I hope he's nice.

Just as I'm thinking that, the door swings open.

I twist around, and, of course, it's Ms. Garcia. She's taller than I expected but looks the same otherwise. Her gray-streaked dark hair is in a neat bun, and she has on a navy-blue business suit.

I notice her royal blue glasses really show off her deep brown eyes when I stand to greet her.

"Hello, Miss Knight," she says, shaking my hand. "How is your first day going?"

"Really well," I reply. "Thank you."

"Please, have a seat." She gestures to my chair as she walks around her desk.

I sit down, as does she, and we begin to review some of the material from the orientation modules. I'm proud of myself that I have good memory retention and am able to answer all of her questions correctly and succinctly.

Leaning back in her plushy desk chair, Ms. Garcia says, "I'm very impressed with your clear work ethic, Miss Knight. And I also don't believe in wasting time. You come to us highly recommended, and I see why. One of your former managers at your intern position in Chicago wrote in his recommendation that you have a 'get it done' attitude and the determination to see any project through to the end, no matter how challenging."

"Wow." Pleasantly surprised at this high praise, I reply, "Thank you."

She nods and goes on. "That being said, you'll be working in the office quite a bit, organizing events, setting up photographers, dealing with the media, that sort of thing. However, I'd also like to put you on a special project for the next couple of months or so."

Intrigued, I tell her, "Oh, okay. I'm up for that."

"Good." She shuffles some papers on her desk. "There's one player who management feels could use a little extra attention. I think you are the absolute right person to help him rebuild and rebrand his image."

Biting my lip, not sure if this is a good thing or not, though it does sound like a challenge, which I'm always up for, I ask, "What exactly would rebuilding and rebranding involve?"

Leaning forward, she temples her hands on the desk and explains, "Essentially the same as we do for all the other players. But, in this situation, we'd like more coverage from the press, more photos, etc. We'll also be setting up extra events for this player. We want to get him out there in the public eye—in a good way, of course. We'll have you involved with the organizing side of things at some point, but for now, your primary duty will be to make sure this player attends and presents the professional image the Thunder expect from every single one of their employees."

Okay, I can do this.

Working with one player might be better than working with a bunch of different ones all the time. I'll get to know my guy personally, meaning we can rebuild and rebrand him to the max.

Amped, I say, "This actually sounds fantastic. I'm ready to start."

"Excellent." Ms. Garcia smiles happily. She jots down a note on a pad on her desk, then, looking up at me, adds, "We have the utmost confidence that you are the best consultant on our team to get this job done. You're new, and this is a perfect opportunity for you to show us what you can do."

"Thank you." I smile back and quickly assure her, "I *can* get this done, and I will. I am the best person for the job."

"Great. That's the attitude we're looking for." Ms. Garcia takes a breath and then says, "I'd like for you to meet with this player tomorrow. Prior to his getting into town, we sent several of his teammates out to deliver digital ticket packages to select season ticket holders. There was one fan, however, that was selected but was out of town. What we'd like to do now is send you and your assigned player over to that ticket holder's house tomorrow afternoon. We have the transportation arranged. You'll leave from here at the arena after practice is over. There's a photographer set up to be on-site to document the delivery and the fan's reaction. Everything is set for this event, so this will be a good opportunity for you and your player to get acclimated to the sort of things that will be expected from this point on."

"Okay." I nod excitedly. "I'll be ready to hit the ground running tomorrow."

"Excellent." Pulling a thick folder from her desk, she passes it over to me. "Here is all the background information you need regarding the player you've been assigned to."

I take the folder, mentally chastising myself that I've been so pumped to have a special assignment that I haven't even thought to ask who my player is.

I hope it's someone good.

Smiling, I glance down at the name on the front of the folder.

Wait…noooo!

This can't be right.

I read the name again—*Hayden Harrington.*

What is the chance?

Though he sure the heck is someone who can use an image polishing.

Still, why does it have to be him?

I glance up at Ms. Garcia, and she, completely unaware I have a problem with this, says, "We feel Mr. Harrington is an excellent choice since you and he both worked for the Blackhawks."

I plaster on a big fake smile and nod.

What can I say? *"No, I can't do this?"*

Certainly not.

So, smiling wide and bright, I tell Ms. Garcia, "Yeah, we did. This is so great."

Great?

Ha, far from it!

But if I value my job—and I certainly do—I better find a way to make this work.

Chapter

Five

HAYDEN

I leave my house early in the morning on Tuesday to head down to the arena for practice. And, as I'm backing my rental SUV out of the garage, I glance over at the house next to mine.

Huh, interesting.

The same beige sedan that was there throughout the weekend is parked once again out in the driveway. Though the car isn't always outside, as there is a garage, clearly someone has moved in next to me.

Like Arden said at lunch, I just hope I have a good neighbor.

Then again, it probably doesn't matter. I've yet to see anyone, so the person must be as busy as I am.

Perfect.

Practice is set to end today at eleven, and then I have an appointment with one of the Thunder's consultants on the player image development team. I was told we'll be heading out to a season ticket holder's house to deliver his digital ticket package. It'll be like a meet-and-greet type of thing.

I was notified late yesterday about the event, and also that I'll be working with this consultant person quite a bit.

I guess the team is looking to rehabilitate my image.

That's okay. I'm on board with that. If I do end up as the first-line center, I'll pretty much be the face of the team.

So, yeah, I need to get this right and play along with whatever the Thunder organization wants.

I just have one hope—that my consultant is cool.

I have another stellar practice, spending most of my time working with Arden and Nils again on the top line.

Though he tries not to show it, I can tell Coach is impressed with my performance. Arden and Nils are happy too.

During our cool-down time on the ice, Nils, skating next to me, says, "Dude, we like Finn, but you *have* to be with us on the top line. There's just no comparison."

"That's what I want," I assure him. "And I'm going to continue to do everything I can to make sure it happens."

I know that means behaving off the ice too.

I can get started on that today.

Yeah, I plan to represent the Thunder in the best way possible for this upcoming fan event.

After my teammates and I leave the ice, we file into the locker room. I take a quick shower, then I dress in nice jeans, running shoes, and a black-and-silver Thunder jersey over a black tech tee.

All set for today's event, I head over to the corporate office area to meet my assigned consultant. My instructions are to meet him or her—I don't even know—in Conference Room B.

I guess we'll leave from there.

When I reach Conference Room B, the door is shut, so I knock on it lightly.

"Come on in," a feminine voice calls out.

Excellent, my consultant is clearly a woman.

I wonder if she's hot.

No, I can't allow thoughts like that to infiltrate my mind.

Best behavior, remember?

Slowly, I open the door, the side of a long table coming into view.

Here we go…

With a friendly, but not flirtatious, smile, I step confidently into the conference room.

And there, standing at the head of the table, wearing a tight black dress I've seen before, is my consultant.

But no, something is different. There's a black blazer over the dress, making it look more professional.

Still, it's the person wearing the dress who has my smile instantly faltering.

You have got to be kidding me.

This cannot be happening.

Why do I keep running into this chick?

At least, now I know why she was on my flight.

I skid to a stop and blurt out, "What the hell?"

"Yeah, that was my initial reaction too," Addison fucking Knight snaps.

She has a smug smile, and her arms are crossed.

Ahh, so she knew before I did that we'd be working together.

But I better check.

Maybe she's in this room for another reason.

Please, God, I hope she is.

With a glimmer of hope sparking to life, I ask, "Are you really my consultant?"

"I really am," she retorts, extinguishing my spark of hope to a burned-out ember. "Look, I'm no happier than you are about this." She sighs. "But this is what the Thunder want, so we may as well make the most of it."

"Easier said than done," I grumble as I head over to the table to sit a few seats down from where she's standing.

I don't want to sit too close; she might bite.

As I scoot my chair in, she sits down.

Opening a file folder, she passes a sheet of paper over to me. "Here is the info on the season ticket holder we're meeting today. He's a middle-aged man named Adam who has two seats in the lower bowl, center ice. He renewed his tickets from last year before the season even ended, so he's obviously a dedicated fan. You'll meet with him and present him his package. It's a nice silver-and-black Thunder-themed box with our signature dark cloud and Thor-like hammer on the lid. Inside, there's a QR code to access his digital tickets and some keepsake promo pieces. The photographer will take a few pics. You'll sign a jersey, and maybe a glossy photo or a puck as well."

"Okay." I nod as I blow out a breath, resigning myself to the fact that this just is what it is, and I can't change it. "Let's do this."

With nothing left to say for now, we proceed out to the shiny black town car that's waiting to take us to the fan's house.

As Addison gets in behind the driver's seat, I slip in the back on the passenger side.

We both practically plaster ourselves to the doors, like we can't put enough space between us.

I'm actually happy when she places her large black work tote in the middle of the seat. A barrier is more than appropriate in this situation.

I'm not planning on making small talk with my nemesis, but curiosity does get the best of me, prompting me to say, "Can I ask you something?"

Flatly, she says, "Sure."

"Did you follow me down here?"

Gawking over at me in disbelief, she snaps, "Are you high?"

"No." I laugh. "I definitely am not."

"Well, then what kind of stupid question is that?"

"A good one," I retort, "seeing as news of the trade was everywhere. You had to have known."

Huffing, she says, "Not that I owe you any sort of an explanation, but yes, I knew the Thunder had picked you up when I accepted the job with them. Sorry to dash your egotistical view of yourself, but it was too good of an opportunity to pass up, even with you in the picture. Also, for the record, the plan was to pretty much avoid you at all costs."

I can't help but let out a loud guffaw. "Ha, well it looks like that plan is shot all to hell. I think we're stuck with each other...at least for a while."

"Ugh," she groans. "Don't remind me. All I know is this is going to be one long-ass beginning of the season."

Damn, she is so fucking right.

Chapter Six

ADDISON

After my heated exchange in the car with Hayden the Horrible, we arrive at the fan's suburban ranch house.

The guy is sweet and happy to be visited by a Thunder player. He's particularly excited that Hayden has joined the team.

At least someone is, right?

Hayden dutifully signs a Thunder jersey and a couple of pucks for the guy, then he meets with his family. The photographer, who was waiting at the house, snaps a bunch of pictures.

All in all, the event is a success.

Hayden is friendly with everyone and, to my surprise, a complete professional. The only thing I hate is that he looks really freaking sexy in his black-and-silver Thunder jersey and jeans.

It kind of softens my opinion of him.

That's why, when we return to the town car, I stop with my hand on the door handle and, peering over the roof, state begrudgingly, "I think that went well. You did a good job, Hayden."

"Thanks," he says, arching a haughty dark brow. "But what did you expect? Did you think I'd act like a caveman or something?"

Jerk!

I almost throw my tote over the roof at him.

So much for softening up; now I'm ready to strangle the man.

Can't he just be gracious for once?

Rolling my eyes, I open the door, jump into the back seat, and slam it shut.

Hayden slips in on the other side, acting like everything is fine.

I let out a snort.

"What?" he asks.

I ignore him, and he shrugs and says, "Fine. Be that way."

This guy.

Glaring over at him, I grind out, "If you must know, I was thinking about your 'caveman' question."

"Oh, yeah?" He cocks his head. "What about it?"

I know I shouldn't, but I can't resist sniping, "I was just thinking that it's a good thing he didn't have an of-age daughter. Then I'm sure your 'caveman' side would have come out, along with, oh let me see"—I tick off—"big-time player, dog, and just general asshat."

Hayden covers his heart, like I just stabbed him with a dagger. "Shit, Knight. You are brutal. But…" He lowers his hand and murmurs grimly, "I shouldn't be surprised."

Oof, low blow.

I guess I had it coming. I mean, I did divulge his secret fling, which led to him being traded. So, yeah, maybe my comment was a little brutal under the circumstances.

Should I tell him I really did it for Kristi?

And that no one expected him to be traded?

I open my mouth to come clean, but just as quickly, I snap it shut.

The reason doesn't matter.

It's probably better to just drop the whole subject.

So I do.

I take out some paperwork from my tote and pretend to review it while Hayden stares out the side window.

I wonder what he's thinking about.

Probably how much he hates me and how us having to work together totally sucks.

Hey, I'm not thrilled either.

But it's my job, and his, too, so what can we do?

I'll just be happy to go home and not have to think about Hayden for what's left of the day.

At least I have that—never having to see or deal with Hayden Harrington at my house.

I sigh, and we sit in silence the rest of the way back to the arena.

Once we're there, without any sort of goodbye or farewell, we go our separate ways.

Hayden heads off to the player parking lot, and I walk to my car in the office employee area.

Once I'm in my rental, I hit the gas and take off.

I can't get away from Harrington, and this whole day in general, fast enough.

Chapter

Seven

HAYDEN

Damn, what a day. Working with Addison Knight is going to be a challenge, that's for sure.

Not that I expected anything less.

Despite our not getting along, the event itself went really well.

That's all that matters.

I did my part, and, to her credit, Addison was completely professional with me in front of the season ticket holder and his family.

There is a silver lining too—I don't have to see Ms. Knight outside of these special promo events, like ever.

I smile at that thought as I pull out of the player parking lot.

What a relief.

Feeling much better and far more relaxed as I drive home, I decide to take my time.

I'm not in any rush, as I have nothing planned but dinner and maybe a little TV.

At the thought of food, my stomach growls.

No surprise since it's past dinnertime, and I never had any lunch.

If I had a different consultant, I would have suggested grabbing a quick bite in an effort to maybe get to know each other a little better.

But I know enough about Addison.

No need to ever break bread with her.

"Fuck, no way."

I pick up some speed, and when I reach the last light before the turn into my neighborhood, I notice a beige sedan in front of me. Since the light is red, I have time to catch that it has out-of-state plates.

Hmmm, must be a rental like mine.

Come to think of it, this sedan looks remarkably similar to the car I've seen parked in the driveway at the house next to mine.

The light turns green, and sure enough, when we reach the entrance to the housing plan, the sedan slows to a crawl and turns.

This has to be my neighbor.

Well, it looks like I'll finally get to see what he or she looks like.

Even though I'm directly behind the car, with the sun going down and the resulting play of shadows and lights, I can't get a clear look at the person driving. Though from the height and slender build, I'm guessing it's a woman.

Wonder what she looks like.

Guess I'll find out soon enough,

We enter the cul-de-sac, and she turns into her driveway.

I pull into mine, but I don't head into the garage. I just park outside, as does she.

Since I'm in a good mood, probably since I'm away from annoying Addison, I decide to be neighborly and head next door to introduce myself.

Okay, I admit it—I really want to see what this chick looks like. Having an attractive female neighbor could end up being a good thing.

A *very* good thing.

Smiling, I make my way up her driveway.

When I'm almost at her car, she opens the door.

I raise my hand to wave and not alarm her as she starts to get out.

But then my smile falters, and I skid to a halt.

No, this can't be right.

Fate would not do this to me.

Damn, it wouldn't do it to us.

Sliding her tote up her shoulder, she turns to close the car door, and that's when she sees me standing there like a creeper.

Shit, this does look weird.

Slamming the car door shut, the sound slicing through the silence like a knife, she snaps, "Harrington, what the hell are you doing in my driveway? This is bizarre. Are you stalking me now? What did you do? Follow me home?"

On the defensive, I snap right the fuck back, "Of course not. And don't get your panties in a bunch."

For that remark, I receive a scowl.

Undeterred, I go on. "I was just coming over to introduce myself. I had no idea *you* are my neighbor. I live next door, by the way."

I wave my hand in the direction of my house, and her big green eyes follow.

When what I'm telling her finally sinks in, she shrieks, "No! You are *not* my neighbor. Tell me this is a nightmare I will wake up from."

I can't help it. I laugh.

I mean, shit, this really is an absurd and strange coincidence.

Still chuckling, I say, "Sorry, but this isn't a nightmare. It's reality. We're neighbors. Unless, of course, one of us decides to move out."

I raise a questioning brow, and she snorts. "Yeah, right. You wish. I'm not going anywhere, pal. I signed a six-month lease."

"Well, so did I, sweetheart. I'm here to stay too."

"Ugh." She leans back on her car, looking suddenly exhausted. "This is unbelievable. You living next to me. What is the freaking chance?"

"Pretty slim, I'd say." I blow out a breath, my anger subsiding. "But here we are."

"Yeah, here we are." She sighs. "So what do we do now?"

"Well…" I cross my arms over my chest. "We can't do anything about having to work together, but we can control what happens here. So how about if we make a deal?"

"What kind of deal?"

"A simple one—I'll leave you alone, and you leave me alone. We'll just do our own thing like the other isn't around. What do you think?"

"I think that sounds perfect," she states.

I raise my brow again, simply because I can tell it irritates the fuck out of her.

"So it's a deal?" I ask.

"Definitely." She nods curtly. "Deal."

I love to push her, so I say, "Should we shake on it?"

I hold out my hand, and she instantly recoils. "Uh, no, I think a verbal agreement is good enough."

"All right, then."

Turning abruptly, she storms off, leaving me in the driveway, hand still out.

So much for having a good neighbor.

I have the worst one possible.

Chapter

Eight

ADDISON

Thankfully, as the week goes by, Hayden and I only have to see each other one time for a quick autograph signing session at a sports store. It's held in an evening and only lasts for one hour, so our interaction is minimal.

We keep it strictly business.

Back at the cul-de-sac that we sadly have to share, we do a great job of avoiding each other. I sometimes catch a glimpse of him getting out of his black Porsche Cayenne, which I assume is his personal vehicle since the rental SUV is gone, but otherwise that's it.

There's a lot of landscaping—shrubs, tall grasses, boulders, and the like—between our properties, so the views are limited.

I did, however, notice that the second-story deck off of my bedroom has a direct line of sight to his deck. I assume that means his house it set up like mine, but switched around, unfortunately making his deck not far from mine.

Hopefully we'll never be out at the same time.

If I do see him out there, I'll just go inside.

That's an easy solution.

"Yep, it sure is," I mutter to myself as I plop down on the comfy beige sofa in the living room.

It's the night before the start of the regular season, so my excitement level is high. I'm about to turn on my laptop to review my work schedule for the upcoming week.

But then Kristi calls on my cell.

I set the laptop aside and pick up my phone from the coffee table.

"Hey, how are you?" I ask.

She says she's good and that she wants to hear how I like Atlanta.

"It seems fine so far," I say. "Though I'm still settling in."

"What about your job?" she asks. "Is it fun? Do you love it?"

"So far I do," I reply truthfully, because besides having to interact with Hayden, it's great. "It's definitely keeping me busy," I tack on.

I fill her in on some details, but I leave out the part about me working exclusively with Harrington.

I just don't want to bring up his name.

But then she asks me directly, "So, have you run into the jerk yet?"

Have I ever.

Quietly, I admit, "Er, yeah, I've seen him around a few times."

I'm not sharing that he lives right next to me. That'll lead to more questions and possibly even her asking me to spy on him or something even worse, like exacting more revenge.

No way.

I'm done with that.

"Huh," she says on a sigh. "I guess that makes sense, you running into him here and there. I'm sure he has to participate in some of the events you're working, right?"

"Um, yeah, he does," I murmur, hoping she'll drop the subject.

I just don't want to talk about Hayden. I've had enough of him. Not to mention, I still don't feel good about divulging their secret fling. As time goes on, and the more I have to think about it, I don't think she should have asked me to get involved in the first place.

But, for my part, I should have said no.

Live and learn, I guess.

To change the subject, I ask her what she's been up to.

To my surprise, she says, "Um, I'm being kind of bad again."

"Wait, what? Again?" My heart sinks. "What does that mean, Kristi? What are you doing?"

Giggling, she says, "I'm dating another player from the team."

Wincing, I ask, "Out in the open, I hope?"

"No way!" she shrieks. "My dad would kill me. You know that."

More likely, he'll have the guy traded.

I beg Kristi, "Please rethink this. You know secret flings do not—I repeat, do *not*—end well. There are consequences."

But there's no changing her mind.

She insists that she knows what she's doing, and that this one won't end badly.

We don't talk that much longer. I'm just not into it after hearing her news, so I tell her I have some work to do online, which is true.

Once we disconnect, I sit and think about how I've learned a new lesson at the age of twenty-four.

Hey, better late than never.

In any case, I know now that I made a mistake back in Chicago. I never should have said a thing about Hayden and Kristi's messy fling. It was not my place, even if, at the time, I thought I was helping out a friend.

Releasing a breath, I vow to stay out of other people's love lives.

And even though mine is currently nonexistent, from this day forward, I promise to only concentrate on my own.

Chapter

Nine

HAYDEN

The first game of the regular season is a home match-up in Atlanta. We're playing the New Jersey Devils.

Wow, and is it ever a lively and raucous crowd! My teammates and I can hear the fans from inside the locker room.

They are pumped.

Good, so are we.

Coach gives us some final rah-rah talk, and we make our way down the tunnel that leads to the ice.

With the lights in the arena flashing and changing colors, the team is introduced one by one.

When it's my turn to take the ice, I'm met with mostly cheers. Though, as I raise my stick and skate around in a circle, I do hear a few boos.

That's okay. I just have to win over the doubters by playing good hockey. Although Addison, and the team, would say I can also improve my image by shining at the promo events.

I'm more interested in the former, especially since I'm in a good position to excel after I did indeed win the top-line spot over Finn.

It was a tough battle, as he was giving it his all, too, but I came out the winner. I worked my ass off at what was left of training camp and scored in our preseason games.

Coach Barnes called me in his office and told me I earned it.

You bet your ass I did, and tonight is my chance to show him he made the right decision.

I get started on doing exactly that when the first puck drops, and I win the face-off. Arden gets the puck, but then a Devils defenseman pokes it away.

From there, both teams do a lot of trapping, making it a tight defensive game.

The first period ends with a score of 0-0.

But then things start to open up a bit in the second.

Deep in the opponent's zone, I handle the puck behind the net, assessing any opportunities.

Nils is in front of the net but heavily covered.

Oh, what the hell?

I try a wraparound goal of my own.

The puck doesn't go in, but it pops out to Nils, who, despite a Devils player hanging all over him, gets a shot in.

Annnnd we score.

Yes!

The boys and I celebrate around the net. It's the first goal of the game and of the season.

And I get the assist.

Coach Barnes pats me on the shoulder when I return to the bench. "Nice play, Harrington," he says.

That makes me feel good.

I don't rack up any more points the rest of the game, but we do win with a score of 3-1.

Everyone is in a good mood in the locker room.

After showering and dressing in the same suits we wore before the game, Arden, Nils, and I head out for a late dinner at a nice, upscale steak restaurant.

"I am fucking famished," I tell the guys as we sit down at a square table tucked away in a quiet corner.

Not that we need the privacy. It's late, and there is only a sprinkling of diners.

Nils and Arden tell me they're hungry, too, so we all order big-ass porterhouse steaks, loaded baked potatoes, and sides of steamed asparagus and broccoli.

When the food arrives, we dig in.

"Damn," Arden says between bites. "This steak is perfect."

"Mine is good too," I reply.

Nils, his mouth full, just nods in agreement.

Once our initial hunger is curbed, we slow down to a more normal eating pace, and a conversation ensues.

We discuss the game, but then, switching gears, Arden asks, "Hey, I've been meaning to ask if anyone moved in next to you."

"Yes." I make a face. "And you're never going to believe who she is."

Arden and Nils both know about my assigned consultant, Addison. I've also filled them in on my history with her. The two of them, who work with different consultants for their promo events— lucky fuckers—think it's pretty bad luck the way things worked out for me.

Ha, just wait until they hear this one.

I haven't even wanted to bring it up. Working with Addison is bad enough. Part of me keeps hoping team management will change their minds.

But no, I think I'm stuck with my enemy.

And now I have to contend with running into her when I'm at home.

Fuck.

Cutting a piece of asparagus, Nils says, "Your neighbor is a 'she,' huh? Is she single? If she is, it can't be all that bad."

"Yeah, for real," Arden agrees. "So who is it? How can it be someone you know when you just moved down here to Atlanta?"

I blow out a breath. "You'd think that would be the case, right? But I know her all too well. She works for the Thunder."

Arden, brows knitting, says, "She does?"

"Yep." I nod once. "And she just so happens to be my fucking consultant."

Arden's mouth drops open, and Nils almost chokes on the asparagus he just popped into his mouth.

"Holy hell," he says once he recovers. "Addison Knight is your neighbor? You're joking, right?"

"I wish I were," I mumble. "But she is indeed my neighbor."

"Man…" Arden shakes his head. "That is some shit luck."

"I know." I set my fork down on the table, suddenly no longer hungry.

"Do you see her a lot when you're at home?" Nils asks.

"No, not really." I shake my head. "We made an agreement to try really hard to stay away from each other."

Arden reminds me, "Yeah, but you still have to attend promo events together."

"Speaking of which," Nils says, "when is your next one?"

"This weekend." I sigh. "I have another autograph signing on Sunday at two o'clock, the day after we return from our away game in Tampa. This one is at a sports store in the mall and will last at least three hours."

"Pfft," Nils chuffs. "That's going to suck. Fly back late on Saturday after the game, and then have to go sign a couple hundred autographs the next afternoon."

Arden, smirking, adds, "All under the watchful eye of your pal, Addison Knight."

I shoot them both the finger. "Thanks, guys. I feel so much better now."

As we share a laugh, the waiter comes by to clear our plates.

After he leaves, Nils says, "Ah, hell, don't sweat it. Maybe you and Addison will come to a truce. And who knows? You may even become friends over time."

He's such an optimist.

"Or—" Arden waggles his brows suggestively. "—maybe something more will develop. I've seen this chick, and she fucking oozes sex appeal. You do know that hate-fucks can be hot, right?"

"That may be true," I begrudgingly agree. "But the day she and I can actually stand each other for more than two seconds, let alone hook up, will be the day hell freezes over. And I think we all know that day will never come."

Chapter

Ten

ADDISON

I watch the first game of the season on the TV in the kitchen while I cut up an assortment of fresh vegetables for a big batch of homemade beef stew I'm making. I figure it will last me through the week for the days I don't feel like cooking or dealing with takeout.

Plus, it's my grandma's recipe and it's freaking delicious.

I made it all the time in Chicago, but this is my first time preparing it here.

I guess I really am settling into my new life.

As I quarter sweet onions, I listen to the TV.

Each player is announced, and when I hear Hayden's name, I stop what I'm doing and look up.

I want to assess the crowd response.

Hmm, he's met with mostly cheers as he takes the ice, raising his stick and skating around. But I also hear a few boos.

That just tells me we have a lot of work still to do.

All the pictures from the ticket delivery event are up on the team website. I also managed to have several of them posted, along with a positive accompanying story, in the local newspaper's online sports section.

The autograph signing session also went well, but it was a short one with not a lot of coverage. We have a longer one this Sunday at a local mall. I'm trying to get the word out on that one. Not only have I set up advertising online, but I've already invited the same photographer from our first event to stop by to document Hayden signing and interacting with fans.

"Small steps," I remind myself as I return to cutting the onions. "We'll get there."

I'm going to make sure Hayden Harrington is loved by all.

Well, everyone but me.

Another good thing is Ms. Garcia is pleased with my progress so far. She's particularly impressed that even when I'm in the office, I'm working diligently on getting the word out about not only Hayden's events but other events for the team, as well.

I should soon be able to set up some of my own.

With all the onions quartered, I add them to the big stockpot on the stove, along with carrots and potatoes I cut up earlier, fresh peas, and big, hearty chunks of beef.

After adding my grandma's secret seasoning and a few other special ingredients, I place the lid on the pot and return to the TV.

Crossing my arms, I watch the opening puck drop.

Hayden wins the face-off.

"Yes," I murmur. "That's how you start the first game of the season. Now let's keep it going."

I can't believe I'm rooting for Hayden, but I have to. Like it or not, he's my player. And if he does his part and plays well, along with stringing together a bunch of successful events, we may actually rehabilitate his image sooner rather than later.

I blow out a breath.

That would be fantastic, as we wouldn't have to work together all that much longer.

Hey, a girl can dream, right?

The next day is beautiful. The sun is shining, the sky is a pretty shade of blue, and the temperature is hovering in the low seventies.

I'm allowed to leave work early, since my BMW is being delivered today. There was a slight weather delay in getting it down here from Chicago, but that's been cleared up, and it's almost here now.

I'm just pumped to get rid of the rental car. I'm anxious to be back in my own familiar vehicle. And I need my other belongings.

Once I'm at my house, but before my car arrives, I change from a business suit to short jean shorts, a soft pink V-neck tee, and white Keds.

It'll be nice to have more of my clothes here, as I'm tired of rotating my suits and one dress for work. I also need more jeans, leggings, and hoodies for when it gets cold. The evenings have already been turning a bit chilly. I suspect, despite the warmth of this afternoon, tonight will be no exception.

As I pad down the stairs, phone in hand, the guy driving my car sends a text that he's about five miles away.

I head straight out to the driveway to meet with him.

I'm not worried about running into Hayden. Practice is a late one today. He probably won't be home for at least a few more hours.

Enough about him, though.

Why is he always intruding into my thoughts?

I guess because I have to work with him, and he just happens to be renting the house next to mine.

I still can't believe that stroke of bad luck.

Keeping my eyes averted from his stupid house, I pace up and down the driveway. Just as I'm kicking a pebble off to the side, I hear a car coming down the cul-de-sac.

I look up to see it's my BMW.

Yay!

The driver, a young guy with reddish hair, pulls into the driveway and up to me. After turning off the ignition, he gets out.

There's some paperwork to sign, which only takes a few minutes, and then he's on his way, chugging off in the ole trusty beige rental.

I'm glad we agreed early on that he'd return it for me.

I decide just to leave my car in the driveway for now, as I have several boxes of clothes to unload, and the front door will provide a quick path to my upstairs bedroom.

I'm thankful it's such a nice day and not raining, as it takes me more trips than I anticipate to lug all the boxes inside, up the stairs, and down the hallway to my bedroom.

When the car is finally empty, I lock up and head inside, closing the front door behind me. I make sure to rearm the alarm, which also locks the door.

With a sigh, I tromp up the stairs, one final duffel bag filled with clothes slung over my shoulder.

Once I reach my bedroom, I drop the bag onto the floor and turn on the lamp on the nightstand.

Daylight is fading.

I hate how the days start to get so noticeably shorter this time of year, like nighttime can't wait to descend.

Flopping down on my back on the bed, I just lie quietly and take a much-needed breather.

"Phew, someone got their workout in today," I murmur as I stare up at the ceiling. "But mission accomplished."

Lifting my head and twisting this way and that, I take in the stacks of boxes around my bed.

I consider unpacking and putting all my stuff away.

But then I figure it can wait.

There's no rush. I can work on putting everything away at my leisure. I mean, it's not like I have a busy social schedule.

"That's sad," I mutter.

But it is what it is.

Blowing out a breath, I decide to quit feeling sorry for myself and just get up and go out onto the deck for a while.

I could use the fresh air.

Once I'm outside, I take a deep breath.

Autumn is definitely in the air.

Though it's still comfortable for the moment, if I plan to chill out here for a while, I may need to dig a hoodie out of one of those boxes.

But not now.

Sighing, I close the sliding glass door, which clicks into place, and then I plop down on one of the comfy cushioned deck chairs.

The view really is nice.

Beyond the small backyard is a tract of land that's heavily forested. The trees are still mostly green, but there's a hint of yellow in some of the leaves.

I also love how quiet it is.

It's peaceful to listen to nothing but the birds singing their lyrical songs as the day comes to a close.

I'm so relaxed that I actually doze off for a bit.

When I wake, the sun is sinking into the horizon, leaving the sky painted in streaks of orange and purple.

It's beautiful, but there is one problem—it's much chillier now than when the sun was high in the sky.

Since I'd like to stay out on the deck a while longer, it's probably time to go in and grab that hoodie.

Rubbing my hands up and down my arms to warm up, I stand and step over to the sliding glass door.

But, shit, I can't open it.

The damn thing is freaking locked.

I wiggle and push and pull but to no avail.

The door is not budging.

Great, I'm stuck outside.

"That must've been the click I heard," I grumble. "I thought the door was just closing, not locking. Shit."

What am I going to do now?

Walking around the perimeter of the deck, I peer over the edges and quickly determine it's way too high for me to jump.

Yeah, a broken leg is the last thing I need.

But I can't stay outside all night. I'm in shorts and a tee. I'll freeze my ass off.

Plus, who's going to save me in the morning?

I can think of only one person who might be able to help—my nemesis neighbor.

Ugh, no.

Slowly, I turn my head and peer over at Hayden's deck.

"Please don't tell me he's my only hope," I mumble.

But he is.

Only problem is I don't even know if he's back from practice.

Even if he is inside his house, what's the chance he'll come out onto his deck?

Pretty slim, seeing as it's getting colder every minute.

Worse yet, it'll be completely dark soon.

"Great."

As the sun dips below the horizon, I consider my options—I can call out for Hayden the Horrible and hope that he hears me, or I can risk turning into a human Popsicle.

Neither option is all that desirable, but my will to survive wins out.

Holding onto the railing of the deck on the side facing his house, I lean over and do something I never thought I'd ever do—I yell for Hayden to help me.

Chapter

Eleven

HAYDEN

Once I'm home after a long and grueling practice, I heat up a grilled chicken breast in the microwave and throw together a salad of mixed greens and fresh vegetables.

When everything is ready, I sit down at the kitchen table and devour my impromptu meal in about seven minutes flat.

Yeah, I was really fucking hungry.

After rinsing off the dishes and loading them into the dishwasher, I decide to go upstairs to unwind and maybe watch a little TV.

In my bedroom, I toe off my slip-on shoes and turn on the big flat-screen on the wall.

But just as I'm about to take off my jeans to get more comfortable, I swear I hear a woman's voice outside yelling, "Help. Help!"

Huh?

I mute the TV.

And then I hear my name.

"Hayden? Hayden, are you over there? Please be home."

Shit, it sounds like Addison.

Is she in trouble?

I may not like her very much, but I'm not going to ignore her if she's in some kind of distress.

No, I'm going to help.

Slipping my shoes back on and sliding open the door leading out to my deck, as her voice sounds like it's coming from the back area of her house, I step outside.

Shit, it's chilly out here.

"Addison?" I call out as my eyes adjust to the darkness.

"Oh, thank God," I hear her say from her deck area. "Hey, I'm over here."

Leaning over my own deck railing, I catch sight of her doing the same on her side.

Hmmm, first thing I notice is she's wearing short-ass jean shorts and a pink tee.

Cute, and definitely sexy, but not very practical.

She waves over to me, and, without thinking, I ask, "What are you doing outside dressed like that? You must be freezing."

She spits out, "No shit, Sherlock." And even from this far apart, I swear I see her rolling her eyes. Exasperated, she adds, "What do you think I'm doing out here? I freaking locked myself out. And I need help. Why else would I be calling for you of all people?"

Okay, even in distress she's quite the smartass.

Crossing my arms, the black material of my long-sleeve tech tee pulling tight across my wide chest, I snark back, "Me of all people, huh? That's not very nice, especially coming from a person in clear need of assistance. Do you want to just stay out there all night? 'Cause I can go back in right the hell now and leave you to your own devices."

Narrowing her eyes at me, she grinds out, "You wouldn't dare."

I'm actually not going to leave her out on her deck to freeze, but, after her snippy remarks, I'm going to let her sweat it out for a minute or two.

So I raise a brow. "Is that a challenge?"

When she doesn't respond, I say, "Okay, then," and pretend like I'm going back inside.

"No, wait," she pleads when I reach for the sliding door handle. "Please, Hayden, don't leave me out here. I could die."

"Hmm," I call back, "that possibility is tempting."

"Stop it!" she yells, stomping her sneakered foot. "This is no time for joking, especially when that could really happen."

There's genuine panic in her voice, so I drop the hard-ass act. "Okay," I say. "I was never going to leave you out here. I was just giving you a hard time."

She sniffs. "Well, it wasn't funny."

"Just…whatever." I shake my head. "Let me come over there, and let's get you back inside your house where I'm sure it's nice and toasty."

"Thanks," she mumbles as she bounces up and down on her toes to try to keep warm.

I start to turn away, but then she calls out, "Wait."

I lean back over the railing. "Yes?"

"How are you going to know which room is my bedroom? You know, to get out here onto the deck?"

"Uh, I think our houses have almost identical layouts, just switched around." I gesture to my sliding door. "The master bedroom over here is connected to my deck also."

That seems to satisfy her, as she nods and says, "Oh, all right.

Makes sense."

"We cool, then?"

"Yeah."

"Okay, give me a sec." I hold up one finger. "I'll be right over."

Bouncing on her toes once more, she says, "Hurry, Hayden."

"I will."

I step inside, closing the sliding glass door behind me.

Since Addison's been outside for a while, I know she's going to need to warm up fast, so I grab a black-and-silver zip-up Thunder hoodie from my closet.

But just as I'm starting out of my bedroom to go rescue her, I remember something.

How will I get in?

Is her front door locked?

Is her alarm armed?

Does she even have an alarm?

I do, so I'm guessing she does too.

"Okay, I better check," I murmur as I head back out onto the deck.

The second Addison sees me, she shrieks, "What are you doing? Are you coming over to help me or not?"

I point at her. "Okay, I'm going to ignore that tone."

"Whatever," she interjects with a huff as she crosses her arms tightly around her torso.

"Ahh, hey, genius," I snap. "There's one little problem we need to address before I rescue your locked-out ass."

"Yeah, what's that?"

"Just how am I supposed to get in? I'm sure your alarm, if you have one, is on, and the front door is locked. All we need is for me to somehow trip the alarm and the police get called out."

She snorts. "At this point, they'd probably get here faster than you."

I cock my head. "Do you want my help or not?"

"I do," she says on a sigh. "And you're right—I do have an alarm, and it's armed. But once you enter the code on the outer keypad— as you probably know, asshat—the front door will automatically unlock."

"Okay, great." I nod, ignoring her snarky insult. "What's the code?"

She hesitates, and, tapping my foot, I say, "Any day now. I'm waiting…"

"Don't you need to write it down?" she asks.

Is she serious?

"How dumb do you think I am?" I ask gruffly. She gives me a do-you-really-want-to-know look, and I hold up my hand. "Don't answer that. Just give me the code, and I, Ugg the Caveman, will try to remember the numbers in my puny brain."

"You said it, not me," she mutters. And then, before I can respond with a witty retort of my own, she mumbles what I think is "8-4-7- 9-6."

"Uh…" I cup my ear. "Can you say it a little louder?"

"But I don't want anyone else to hear," she protests.

"Seriously?" I make a sweeping motion with my hand. "We're the only ones around, sweetheart. Who in the hell is going to hear? Our neighbors a block away? Do you think they have bionic ears?"

"Oh, shut up, Harrington," she grumbles. "Are you ready?"

I tap my foot. "I was born ready, honey."

"You're so weird," she says as she rolls her eyes at me again. But then, this time loud and clear, she calls out, "8-4-7-9-6."

I nod. "Got it."

Repeating the numbers in my head, I start on my way over to the monster Addison's lair, where I hope she doesn't slay me.

Chapter

Twelve

ADDISON

While I wait out on my deck, shivering by this point, I think about how I actually am grateful Hayden is coming to save my ass.

And what a cold ass it is at the moment.

I should probably be a little nicer to the man, but bantering with him is far too much fun.

I just can't help myself sometimes.

Oh, well, he seems to enjoy it too.

And he certainly has some good comebacks.

I have to respect him for that, though I don't want to.

I mean, I'm supposed to hate the guy, right?

Maybe "hate" is too strong of a word.

I don't know.

I think the cold is getting to me, freezing my brain or something.

Sighing, I plop down and curl up on the deck chair with the

plushy cushions, tucking my legs under my body in an effort to warm up.

Hayden is actually pretty quick in getting over to my house.

Still, when he opens the sliding glass door and steps out onto the deck, I can't resist staring up at him and saying, "Finally."

I swear there's a smile tugging at his full lips as he volleys back, "You're welcome, sweetheart."

Standing and rolling my eyes, I tell him, "Quit referring to me with terms of endearment. We don't even like each other, you know?"

For this one long beat, our eyes meet.

Damn, his blues are pretty, even in the moonlight.

Wait, what am I thinking?

But I can't stop.

He holds my gaze, and I bite my lip.

For a second or two, there's this connection. One where there's no hate or dislike, but definitely attraction.

It's nice.

I like it.

He breaks the moment, though, when he holds out a hoodie.

Flustered, I say, "What's that for?"

"It's for you, silly. Now put it on."

"Silly?" It's my turn to cock a brow at him. "Seriously?"

"Hey, you said no more terms of endearment, so 'silly' it is."

"You are such a child," I mutter.

Waving the hoodie at me, he says, "Just put this on already. And let's get inside. It's fucking cold out here."

"I think I'm getting used to it," I lie.

"Addison, I swear..."

"Okay, all right." Blowing out a breath, I snatch the hoodie from him and shrug it on and zip it up.

The damn thing is way too big, as it's clearly his, but that just makes it all the warmer, seeing as it practically reaches my bare knees.

It also smells kind of good—soapy and manly.

I have a sudden, inexplicable urge to lift my arm and take a deep whiff, but I'll be damned if I'm going to sniff Hayden's hoodie in front of him. I'd never hear the end of it.

Staring at me like he's trying to figure out what's going on in my mind—*he can never know I like his manly scent*—he says, "Come on. Let's go in."

"Okay." I nod.

Once we're in my bedroom, I close the sliding door, where it locks once again automatically.

Watching me, Hayden says, "There's a small lever off there to the side. Mine is the same. You have to disengage that so it doesn't lock every time it's closed. I just keep mine in the position where you can lock and unlock it as you please."

"Ah, that's a good idea." I find the lever and disengage it. Then I lock the door manually. "What a stupid feature," I grumble as I turn back to him.

"It is," he agrees. "If I owned the house, I'd have it changed. But I don't, so what can you do?"

He shrugs, and I nod. "Yeah, I guess just be careful is all."

"For sure."

Out of words, we just stand here and stare at each other.

Hmmm, his eyes are even prettier in the low light from the lamp, like a pale, pale blue.

It's funny, because I try not to pay attention to things like his gorgeous eyes and how good-looking he is when we're working together.

But here alone with him in my bedroom, I can't help myself.

Maybe he's doing the same?

I mean, when he tears his gaze from mine, I catch him sneaking a glance down to my legs.

But this has to stop.

"Um…" I release a breath. "I should, uh, walk you downstairs. I'm sure you want to get back over to your house."

"Yeah." He nods, raking his hand through his hair. "I should get going."

We head down the hall and the stairs in silence.

At the front door, I start to unzip his hoodie.

"Oh, here," I say. "I'm sure you want this back."

"No, that's okay." He holds up his hand. "Just keep it for now. You can give it back to me whenever."

It is kind of comfy and warm, so I nod. "All right. Thanks."

"No problem."

He turns and places his hand on the doorknob, preparing to leave, but I stop him. "Hey, Hayden."

He turns back to me. "Yeah?"

As sincerely as I can, I tell him, "Thank you. You know, for saving me tonight. I don't know what I would have done. I guess break the glass or freeze for real. Either option wouldn't have been a good one, though. So, yeah, thank you."

In a tone devoid of any sarcasm or venom, he replies, "You're welcome, Addison."

And then he's gone.

Before I go up to bed, I lean back against the closed front door and think about a nice way I can repay him.

Maybe tomorrow morning, before I go to work, I'll take over some of my grandma's secret recipe beef stew.

Yeah, that would be perfect.

Smiling, and for the first time feeling kind of okay about Hayden Harrington, I head up to bed.

Chapter

Thirteen

HAYDEN

The next morning, just as I'm about to leave the house for practice, the doorbell rings.

Imagine my surprise when I open the door to find Addison on my front steps.

Her tote is slung over one shoulder, and in the other hand, she's holding a plastic container filled with something that looks like soup.

"Hi," she says with a smile.

"Hey." I nod, barely noticing that she's now holding the plastic container out to me.

Yeah, I'm far too distracted by how absolutely pretty she looks this morning. Her long raven hair is a mass of soft curls tumbling over one shoulder, and her eyes look especially green in the bright daylight.

Maybe it's also because she has on a fuzzy kelly green sweater. It really brings out the color of her eyes. It's just the right amount of snug too. And the black pencil skirt she's wearing further accentuates her sexy curves.

I'm not even normally a shoe guy, but her black patent leather pumps with little green bows that match her sweater just add to her overall allure.

Damn, this woman is hot.

Too bad we don't get along.

Though last night wasn't too bad, particularly not at the end. It was like we reached an unspoken truce of some sort.

"Hayden, are you okay?" she asks, tilting her head and peering at me curiously.

I chuckle and reply, "Yes, I'm fine. I'm just surprised to see you on my doorstep, that's all."

Um, even though it's the truth, maybe it's not the best thing to say.

Pulling back the container sharply, she mutters, "This was a bad idea."

"Wait, what?" I try to apologize. "I didn't mean that in a bad way. I'm just surprised, okay?" I wave my hand. "You know what? Never mind. Can we just start over?"

She sighs. "Yes, sure, I guess." Holding the container out to me once more, she says, "I made homemade beef stew the other day. I have more than enough, so I thought I'd bring some over as a thank-you for helping me out last night."

Ah, so it's stew, not soup.

I take the container and hold it up to my nose. Even though there's a plastic lid creating a strong seal, I detect the hint of a delicious beefy aroma.

"Mmm, smells good," I say. "Looks like I know what I'll be having for dinner later today."

Looking pleased, Addison shares, "It's my grandma's recipe. I had some the other night after it was done, and, if I do say so myself, I think it turned out pretty good."

"I'm sure it's delicious," I reply as I lean back in the doorway so I can set the stew on a nearby stand. "Thank you."

She swishes her hand in the air. "It's not that big of a deal, Hayden. But you're welcome." Turning like she's about to leave, she falters and murmurs, "Crap."

"What?" I ask.

"I forgot your hoodie. I meant to give it back, but I left it up on my bed."

Before I can censor myself, I raise a brow and say, "On your bed, huh? Did you sleep in it?"

I really, really, for some reason, want her to say yes. And though she doesn't confirm or deny, I can tell by the way she starts blushing like crazy that she actually fucking did.

Holy hell!

"You did, didn't you?" I say, again without thinking. "Or you thought about it, huh? Am I right?"

Shit, now she's mad.

Crossing her arms and shooting me a look of disgust, she snaps, "I most certainly did not sleep in your hoodie *or* think about doing such a thing. I simply set it on the bed this morning so I wouldn't forget it."

"Ah, but you did forget it, eh? Maybe that was on purpose. Subconsciously, you know?"

"Have you lost it?" she asks as she gawks at me like I have.

"No." I shake my head. "Not at all. But maybe you have."

Damn, I can't stop digging my own grave. So much for our shaky truce. That shit just crumbled all to hell.

"You know what?" She starts tapping her foot. "I think I'll just take that stew back."

"What?" I scoff as I block the door, like she might be serious enough to barge in and grab the container from the stand I set it on. "No way, babe. You gave it to me. Not to mention, I thought it was your way of saying 'thank you.'"

"It is," she says, capitulating. "I didn't really mean that." She waves her hand. "Just keep it, okay?"

She seems calmer now, like she's given up.

Good, I like to win.

And because of that desire for victory at all costs, even in this dumb spat, I can't resist getting the last word in.

Snarkily, I bite out, "Wait, I don't know if I want to keep your stew after all. Are you sure you didn't poison it or something? I could see you doing that."

Without missing a beat, she volleys back, "You know what? I should have poisoned it. Then I'd never have to see your stupid face ever again."

"Stupid?" I snort as I run my hand down my smoothly shaved cheek. "I've been told it's a nice face. It's soft this morning too. Do you want to touch it and see for yourself?"

"Ugh, you...you...you wish."

She's spitting mad now.

"What?" I act all innocent. "Is it something I said? Or maybe it just bothers you that you really do want to touch me."

Angrily, she retorts, "You are such an arrogant ass. I really can't stand you. I wouldn't touch you if my life depended on it. I wish you hadn't even helped me last night."

"Really?" I laugh. "Then you'd still be out there on the deck, probably frozen."

"Who cares?" she yells. "At least then I wouldn't be dealing with your annoying ass."

"Ah, but I think you like dealing with my ass, annoying or not."

"Just shut up, Hayden." Spinning on her heels, she takes off.

But as she stomps down my walkway, I can't resist putting on my most sugary-sweet tone and calling out, "See you Sunday for the autograph signing. I can't waiiiittt."

Without turning back, she holds up her hand and promptly gives me the finger.

Later that day, after practice ends, I return home and warm up some of the stew Addison gave me.

It turns out to be fucking delicious. And it's clearly not poisoned, not that I really ever believed it was. I was just being a dick. I actually feel kind of bad for sparring with her this morning.

How did it even start? I wonder as I sit at the kitchen table and dig my spoon into my bowl of stew.

As I devour the last hearty bite, I remember my hoodie comment was the truce-breaker.

I should have kept my mouth shut. At this point, she'll probably burn my hoodie and I'll never see it again.

"I like that one too," I mumble as I push the bowl away and lean back in my chair. "Oh, well."

I consider going next door to apologize, but it's only a little after two. I'm sure Addison is still at work.

I didn't see her car, which is a white BMW, no longer the beige rental, out in the driveway. It could be in the garage, but I don't think so. We both seem to park outside a lot.

It's fine that she's not home. It's probably best to just let this go. I'll be away for a couple of days, anyway.

Our team leaves for Tampa tomorrow afternoon for an away game with the Lightning on Saturday.

Looks like I'll just deal with Addison and the fallout from our argument on Sunday at the autograph signing.

That is, if she's even still talking to me.

Chapter

Fourteen

ADDISON

I swear Hayden Harrington is going to be the death of me.

"And if he doesn't take me out," I murmur as I close my eyes and slide down deeper into the steamy, hot bubble bath I drew for myself a short while ago, "I very well might end him."

Before I do, though, I'd like to feel his full lips pressed to mine. Just once. They look so soft and luscious all the time.

Mmm, and I bet they'd feel even better right—I trail my fingers up along my inner thigh—*here.*

Wait, no.

I stop and sit up straight, water and bubbles sloshing over the side of the tub.

"I am not doing this. Not with that asshat in the starring role." I cross my arms to make sure I don't waver and give in.

It's late Saturday night, and I can't believe I was just about to touch myself while thinking about Hayden.

Sighing, I pull the plug, allowing the bubbly water to drain. Shaking my head, I stand and dry off, before heading into my bedroom with a towel wrapped around me.

I shouldn't have watched the game earlier this evening. Hayden played exceptionally well and looked even better, especially when he took off his helmet over on the bench midway through the third period to adjust a strap.

He was all hot and sweaty…in a very sexy kind of way.

That's what put these crazy ideas in my head in the first place. I had a thought about how that probably is the way he looks when he's on top of someone, pounding away.

And here's that thought again.

Oh, my…

Ugh, stop.

But I can't.

I'm just too worked up.

So I give in.

I'll think of him only this once to get him out of my system.

Dropping the towel, I slip on Hayden's hoodie, which still totally smells like him.

I then do the unthinkable—I lie down on my bed and touch myself as I think about engaging in the dirtiest things with the man I love to hate.

On the way to the autograph signing on Sunday afternoon, I am beyond happy that Hayden and I agreed when the event was set up to just meet at the mall.

After last night, I'd die of embarrassment if I had to sit next to him in a car.

Getting through this event is going to be rough enough.

I finally came to my senses—after three mind-blowing orgasms, by the way—and vowed to never get off ever again while thinking about Hayden and all the hot things we could do together to release our pent-up anger toward each other.

I even hid his hoodie in the back of my closet so I won't be tempted to put it on again.

Yeah, leaving it draped over the back of a chair near the bed was not a good idea. I was even going to bring it today to give it back to him, but I was worried that, after last night, it'd smell more like a fresh-out-of-the-shower me than him.

He might figure it out then—that though I hate him, I lust over him and did some dirty things in his hoodie.

We can never let him learn that annoying little fact.

The man is smug and arrogant enough as it is.

If he knew he starred in my fantasies, even once…

Oh, God.

I shudder.

He can never know that.

By the time I reach the mall, I'm downright mad—at myself, and at Hayden, generally for just existing.

I slam my car door shut, button the jacket part of my black business suit, then tromp into the mall. I head straight to the sporting goods store where the signing is being held, my heels clicking loudly on the glossy mall floor.

I pass a long line of fans, and an employee lets me into the store, ushering me to the back, where a table is set up for Hayden to sign the autographs.

I check my phone and see we have about fifteen minutes until the doors open and we let the fans in.

I'm calmer now, but I'm quickly back to my state of irritation when Hayden arrives through a back door and a) he looks amazingly hot in a dark gray suit, and b) his very presence makes me think about what I did last night.

Worse yet, I kind of want to do it again.

"What's up your ass?" he asks when he steps toward the table, and I brush past him to place a bunch of Sharpies next to a pile of eight-by-ten glossy photos of him on the ice in his uniform.

"*You* are what's up my ass," I snap without even thinking about how that sounds.

Shit.

I mentally smack my forehead.

Grinning, he steps closer to me and murmurs in a husky tone, "That could be arranged. Would you like that, Addison? You strike me as the kinky type."

Gulp.

"Get away from me," I hiss, "before I call and report you to human resources."

He stumbles back so fast it's like I slapped him.

Feeling bad, because this is just what we do all the time, I tell him, "I wasn't serious. I'm sorry."

"It's fine." He starts messing with the Sharpies, careful not to make eye contact with me. "I apologize as well. What I said was inappropriate."

I release a frustrated breath. "Aw, man, we are just never going to get along, are we?"

Finally raising his eyes to meet mine, sadness in his pretty pale blues, Hayden states matter-of-factly, "Probably not."

I just shake my head before I walk away to talk to the

photographer, who just arrived.

When the event gets underway, it's like nothing ever happened. Hayden signs a ton of autographs and takes several selfies with fans, his smile and interactions all genuine.

I also am professional. I check in with the photographer on shots I'd like for him to get, and I make sure Hayden is comfortable.

When he needs water, I get it for him.

When the glossy photos of him run out, I replace them with more.

When he needs to take a bathroom break, I keep the fans occupied by passing out complimentary magnetic team schedules.

Everything runs so smoothly that the hours fly by.

The line dwindles, and Hayden signs a final few autographs.

The store then closes its doors, and the photographer leaves.

We begin to wrap up.

I notice there's only one employee remaining, and he's giving us a lot of space. That's good; it means we can talk.

"That went well," I say to Hayden as I collect the markers and the remaining photos to place in my tote.

"I think so too," he agrees as he shrugs on the suit jacket he took off about halfway through the event when it got too warm in the store.

He's being cordial, so I think our earlier argument is forgotten.

In an effort to keep the peace, I say, "You were so nice to everyone. I think they all felt like they got to know you a little better as a person, not just as a player."

"I'm just playing the game, Addison," he says with a shrug. "Just playing the game."

I cross my arms and level him with a stern look. "Is that all you think this is?"

"Isn't it?" He raises a brow. "I'm just trying to do what I need to do to get out of this arrangement of ours. 'Cause it sure feels like that's all *we* are ever doing. Playing games."

Damn, I don't want it to be this way. I want to have a good professional relationship with Hayden. I'm sure Ms. Garcia expects nothing less. But it seems like our animosity is starting to spill over into work.

I have to own up, though, that today I was the one who started it. That's why I need to fix it.

Sighing, I uncross my arms and ask Hayden, "Can we call a truce?"

Holding the back of the chair tucked under the signing table, he says, "I thought we had sort of an unspoken one after I saved your ass."

I let his smartass comment slide and reply quietly, "I thought so too."

"So what happened?"

I laugh. "Do you really think we should rehash it? That'll probably start another fight."

"Yeah." He chuckles. "You're right. So what do we do now?"

"We call a new truce and start over…again."

"Okay." He nods. "I can do that."

"Good. So can I." I hold out my hand. "Should we shake on it this time?"

"Sure."

We didn't last time, nor did we shake hands when we agreed to avoid each other.

And look how that all turned out.

Yeah, it's time to try a new tactic.

He takes my hand, and as my skin touches his, we hiss in

simultaneous breaths.

Damn, there is some crazy-wild electricity between us.

"Addison," he breathes, releasing his grip.

"I know." Averting my eyes, I pull away my hand. "Just…umm…"

Quickly, he says, "I'm sure that jolt, or whatever it was, is because we fight all the time."

"Yeah." I nod vigorously. "That has to be it."

Looking worried, he asks, "Our truce is still on, though, yeah?"

"It is, yes, absolutely."

The truce is still on, but we dare not shake on it again.

Chapter

Fifteen

HAYDEN

After we agree to a new truce, as time goes by, a funny thing happens—Addison and I start to get along.

I don't know if it's purely for professional reasons or because we're both so competitive that no one wants to be the first to fuck it up, but we're actually not at each other's throats every minute.

I like it.

It's good.

We say hello now when we run into each other back at our houses, and that's fairly often. There are no more "avoidance" games.

We just live life like normal.

We're also much kinder to each other.

Like the other day, I returned her container to her and was sure to let her know how much I loved the stew, which was totally true.

That seemed to please her.

"I can make it again sometime," she said. "And share some with you, of course."

"I'd like that," I told her.

We had kind of a moment then, as I stood on her doorstep. She leaned against the frame, and her eyes held mine.

I smiled softly. "So…," I murmured.

"Yeah?"

Right then the mailman arrived, and, just like that, the moment passed. I don't know what I was going to say anyway. It's probably for the best that we were interrupted.

Oh, and one more thing…

Addison stopped by my house one afternoon to finally give me back my hoodie.

Weird thing, it smelled like her.

I just know she was sleeping in it…or doing something else while wearing it.

Shit, I can't think about the latter—it makes my dick hard. That can't happen, as we're supposed to be strictly friends and business associates.

Speaking of work, our events all go smoothly. We behave more like partners now, not adversaries.

Things really have changed.

So much so that from time to time, we even share a laugh or two.

Addison loves hearing stories of how we hockey players like to play jokes on one another.

The other day, when we were in her office going over the schedule of upcoming promo events, I told her about this one time, after a big snowstorm and when I was playing in Chicago, a bunch of us built an impenetrable snow fort around the captain of our team's car.

"You should have seen the look on his face when he came out and saw his car was surrounded by a snow wall," I shared, chuckling.

"Oh my God, Hayden." Addison laughed. "What did the poor guy do?"

I shrugged. "Eh, what could he do? He borrowed a shovel from maintenance and dug his car out. It took him, like, an hour. Man, it sure was a classic prank."

"Yeesh, you guys." She shook her head. "Did he ever get any of you back for what you did?"

"Er, um…" I trailed off, not wanting to share how he paid me back.

He was the one who set me up with the coach's daughter—knowing full well I'd be toast if her dad ever found out. I don't think he ever intended for me to get traded, though.

Sometimes pranks go too far.

When Addison pressed for details of the captain's payback, I just told her I didn't remember what he did.

Thankfully, she let it go, like a real friend would do.

"Shit," I mutter softly as I'm driving back to my house from the airport. We had a late game in Pittsburgh last night and flew back early this morning. "Are Addison Knight and I slowly becoming true friends?"

I chuckle because, yeah, I think we kind of are.

No, I know we are.

For some reason, that puts me in a really good mood. I don't even care all that much that we lost the game last night. We still have a winning record six weeks into the season.

That's a good start.

As I approach my house, I notice Addison is out by her front door. She's in black leggings and a gray sweatshirt, and her long hair is up in a high ponytail.

She also appears to be struggling with a huge box.

Instead of pulling into my driveway, I cruise into hers, the recently fallen leaves crunching beneath my tires.

Powering the passenger-side window down, I lean over the console and say, "You look like you could use some help with that thing."

"Hayden." She blows out a relieved breath, lifting a wisp of dark hair that fell out of her ponytail and onto her cheek. "I sure as hell could use a hand. This box is heavy as shit."

I hop out and stride over, nodding to the bulky box. "What's in there, anyway?"

"It's an exercise bike. I thought with winter coming, it'd be a great way to stay in shape."

I almost blurt out that she's already in amazing shape, but I figure that may be misconstrued as flirtatious. That is one thing we're careful about, not flirting, especially after the last time our skin touched and it was pure electricity.

I think neither of us wants to mess up our truce and newfound friendship.

Running my hand through my hair to clear my wayward thoughts, I note, "There's no way that bike is assembled. Though the box is huge, it's not big enough."

"No." She shakes her head. "It's not."

Taking hold of the box and lifting it with ease, I ask her, "So who's going to put this thing together?"

She pops open the front door and shrugs. "Um, I don't know. I guess me."

"Do you have tools?" I grunt out as I bring the box into the house and set it just inside the door.

Pondering, she says, "There are probably some in the basement."

"Yeah, maybe." I place one hand on top of the box. "But if you need any, I know for sure there are a lot over at my house."

Her vibrant green eyes light up. "Ooh, could you bring some over just in case? Also, I really don't even know what I need." She hesitates, and then adds, "I mean, when you have a chance. I know you just got back from an away game last night."

Tapping the top of the box, I tell her, "No worries. It's Saturday, so I actually have nothing to do today. Let me just head over to my house, change my clothes"—I gesture to the navy-blue suit I have on—"and grab some tools. I'll move this box to wherever you want to place the bike. And, if you'd like me to, I can help you put it together."

Breathing out a clear sign of relief, she says, "That would be amazing. I'm really not that great with assembling stuff. I'm willing to try, but you helping would make it so much easier."

"Yeah, I bet." I laugh.

I have a feeling I'll be doing most all of the work.

But that's okay.

I wouldn't have offered if I didn't want to help.

So I add, "Don't worry. I'll help you, Addison." I start for the door. "Give me about half an hour or so, and I'll be back over."

"Great." She nods excitedly. "I'll be ready."

I start to leave, but then she stops me. "Oh, hey, Hayden."

I turn around. "Yeah?"

"Thank you."

At my house, I change into old, faded jeans and a snug black T-shirt. After slipping on a pair of athletic shoes and grabbing a box of tools from the garage, I make my way back over to Addison's place.

She greets me at the door and shows me where she wants the

bike to be set up, which is smack-dab in the middle of the living room.

"Are you sure you want it right here?" I ask as I push the coffee table out of the way and set the box between the sofa and the love seat. "There's a game room downstairs, right? That probably wouldn't be as cramped."

She shakes her head, her long ponytail swinging. "No. It's not like I'm entertaining in this room anyway. And when I want to watch TV, I can ride the bike." She points to the big flat-screen on the wall. "There's not one of those down in the game room."

"Okay." I start to open the box. "That makes sense. I'll assemble the bike here, but, if you want, I can move the furniture around so it's arranged like it was but a little off to the side some. The bike can sit behind the love seat, and you'll still have a good view of the TV."

Pleased, she replies, "That sounds perfect."

With a nod, I get started.

As I suspected, I end up doing most of the work. Though, to her credit, Addison does hand me pieces of the bike and different tools I ask for.

Partway through the assembly, she wants to know if I'd like something to eat.

I think it over. "Hmm, I am kind of hungry."

Standing, she asks, "Are sandwiches all right? I have roast beef or smoked turkey."

"Either is fine with me." I set down a wrench and pick up a screwdriver. "Why don't you surprise me?"

"Okay." She pauses for a beat. "Oh, is there anything you don't like on your sandwich?"

"Just no mustard." I shudder. "Anything else is fine."

"Not a problem," she says with a laugh. "There's no mustard in this house. I hate it too."

As I tighten a screw, I murmur, "Ahh, I knew there was a reason why I like you so much."

She's quiet, and I'm worried that I just said the wrong thing.

But when I look up, she's smiling.

Softly, she says, "I kind of like you a lot, too, these days, Hayden. Like for real, no joke."

Laughing, I shake my head. "It's amazing, huh?"

"How do you mean?"

"Just… Who would have thought we'd ever say we actually *like* each other? I guess our truce is working, huh?"

"Yeah." Still smiling as she turns to head to the kitchen, she agrees cheerfully, "It totally is."

Chapter

Sixteen

ADDISON

As I scamper off to the kitchen, I'm thinking two things—how happy I am that our truce is working, and that I really need to stop lusting over Hayden.

He, of course, has no clue that I think he's so damn freaking sexy.

Speaking of which, why must he look so fine in old, faded jeans and a black tee that shows off his hard body and defined muscles?

Not that I was looking at those muscles, flexing and bulging, as he was putting together my exercise bike.

Okay, I totally was.

I was trying not to, as I don't want to mess up what we're building—a friendship. Getting along with Hayden is so much better than fighting with him all the time.

I mean, hell, if we were still at odds, he wouldn't be putting my bike together. And it surely would have taken me days to assemble the damn thing. Even then, it probably wouldn't have been right.

I'd probably have sat on it for the first time and ended up on the floor.

After it collapsed, of course.

So, yeah, much like rescuing me from the deck, Hayden has saved me once again.

To show my gratitude, I make him an amazing sandwich. I toast the whole grain bread to perfection and pile on loads of roast beef, provolone cheese, Bibb lettuce, tomato slices, and a smear of mayo.

I even place a dill pickle spear on the side of the plate as a garnish.

Yeah, we're getting fancy here.

Chuckling, I make my sandwich the same way, but Hayden's is much bigger.

Hey, he said he was hungry.

When I head back into the living room and hand him his plate, his eyes widen. "Wow, now this is a sandwich."

Taking a seat on the sofa, I set my own plate on my lap. "I hope you like it."

"I'm sure I will," he says as he lifts the sandwich to his luscious mouth.

Okay, stop it, Addison.

After taking a substantial bite, then chewing and swallowing, he says, "I love it. This is delicious. Good job."

"Thanks," I murmur.

Hayden takes a break from working on the bike and joins me on the sofa to finish his lunch.

As we eat quietly, I think of something I've been meaning to ask him.

Swiping my mouth with a paper napkin, I say, "I know you obviously lived in Chicago for a while, but where are you from originally?"

For some reason, I want to know more about him. The file Ms. Garcia gave me is filled with mostly just hockey-related info.

"Buffalo, New York," he says around a mouthful of sandwich.

"Huh, interesting. What about family? You were never married, were you?"

That makes him laugh. "No. Were you?"

"No." I then ask, "What about siblings? Do you have any?"

After he swallows another bite of sandwich, he says, "I have one older brother. He lives in Buffalo still. He's a great guy. He teaches and coaches high school hockey. What about you? Where are you from? And do you have any brothers or sisters?"

I nod. "I have one sister. Her name is Willow, and she's a year younger than me. We're from Pennsylvania, a little town north of Pittsburgh. It's called Butler."

He laughs. "No way. You're from the Pittsburgh area? I guess you were happy last night when the Penguins won."

I shake my head. "Nope. Though I still like them and root for them any other time, not when they are playing us. I'm an Atlanta Thunder fan first. They're my number one team."

He pumps his fist in the air. "Fuck yeah! That's what I like to hear." Setting his plate on the end table on his side of the sofa, he wipes his mouth with his napkin and then asks, "So, tell me how you ended up working for the Blackhawks."

This is an easy one.

Releasing a breath, I say, "Well, I had just finished an accelerated MBA from the University of Chicago, and the internship with the Blackhawks opened up. I love hockey and wanted to get into sports marketing, so it was a no-brainer."

"Nice."

Hayden grows quiet and appears to be lost in thought, so, after setting my plate on the end table on my side, I ask him, "What are you thinking?"

"Ah, no, it's nothing." He waves his hand dismissively. "I don't think it's something I should bring up."

"Oh, come on." I crumple up and throw my napkin at him. "Now you have to tell me."

"Okay, okay." Chuckling, he rests his arm on the back of the sofa and twists to face me. "It's just…" He picks up the napkin I tossed at him and toys with it. "I've always wondered why you told on me. You know, about… Well, you know."

Yeah, I know exactly what and who he means. I still feel rotten about the whole thing, and I need for him to know that.

Running my hand down my face, I groan. "Ugh, yes, that. I knew it'd come up eventually." My eyes meet his. "First off, I'm sorry, Hayden. I never should have said anything. I thought you'd broken Kristi's heart, and not that it's even a good excuse, but I got too involved and caught up in it all."

"She knew what she was doing," he says quietly. "And, for the record, I never meant to hurt anyone."

I blow out a breath. "I know that now. And I don't want to throw anybody under the bus, but you should know the truth—*she's* the one who asked me to say something."

His brows fly up. "You're kidding me."

"No." I shake my head. "But I still own it fully. I did it, not her. But I know now that I should have refused. At the time, I felt bad for her and wanted to be a good friend. Still, it was a stupid thing to do without having all the facts or realizing what could happen. The crazy thing is, ever since I moved down here to Atlanta, I never even talk to her anymore. We talked once early on, and I've tried since then to text and call, but I think she's kind of ghosted me."

I leave out the part about her telling me she's messing around with another player. Not that he'd care. It's just not my story to tell, and I've learned my lesson to keep out of other people's business.

Look at the harm I did to Hayden.

"Well," he sighs, running his hands down his jean-clad thighs. "Friendships are like that sometimes. Not every relationship lasts forever."

"No, that's true." I look over at him and ask softly, "So, do you forgive me?"

He smiles. "Sure, yeah, I do. I understand everything now. You were just trying to be a good friend and got caught up in something that spiraled out of control."

"That's for sure." I snort. "Still, I hate how it all went down."

"Hey." He waves his hand in the air. "It's water under the bridge, okay? It all worked out for the best anyway. I'm a top-line center on a team that's playing pretty damn well."

"Good point," I agree, relieved he feels this way. "And you really are playing next level."

"I'm trying," he says.

With the Kristi issue resolved, Hayden slips back down to the floor to get back to work on the bike.

And I, feeling better than I have in a long time about what happened in Chicago, take our empty plates into the kitchen.

Now the past really is in the past, and Hayden and I can move forward with our friendship.

Chapter

Seventeen

HAYDEN

After Addison explains why she busted on me about my fling with Kristi, everything makes more sense. I wasn't really harboring any resentment toward her anymore, anyway.

I was more just curious.

Still, I'm glad I know the full story.

Damn Kristi, too scared to tell on me herself.

Oh, well.

Whatever.

Like I told Addison, it's all working out for the best. The team is happy with my progress—both on the ice and off.

A couple days after I assemble Addison's exercise bike, she calls me from work.

"Hey," she says. "I have great news."

I'm on my way to meet Arden for lunch, but I'm early, so I make the turn into the restaurant parking lot and pull into an empty spot.

Cutting the ignition but leaving the phone synced to the car speaker, I say, "Yeah, what kind of great news?"

"The really great kind," she says, sounding über-pumped.

"Well, spill it, girl."

Barely able to contain her enthusiasm, she says in an excited rush, "I got you a sit-down interview with *Atlanta Sports Monthly*. You're going to be the feature for January. You get the cover and everything, Hayden. This is beyond amazing."

I'm floored, in the best kind of way. "Wow. That is fucking fantastic."

This really is big, and I'm excited. *Atlanta Sports Monthly* is next-level media. They have a national following and only feature big-name athletes.

And the cover and feature story?

Damn.

Addison is vibrating with as much energy as I'm feeling. It's coming through the speaker, especially when she squeals, "I know, right?"

"Wow," I go on, still amazed. "How did you land that?"

"I don't know." I imagine her shaking her head, trying to be humble. "I just went after it. I guess I talked to the right people and pleaded my case strongly enough. Well, your case, actually."

I laugh. "You must've really talked me up."

"I did." She sounds excited, and that touches my heart. "I told them to watch out for Hayden Harrington, in a good way, and that you're on the verge of breaking out."

Softly, I murmur, "I hope you're right, Addison."

"I am," she insists. "Look at your stats so far. You're leading the team in points."

Now it's my turn to be humble. "Yeah, I guess I am."

She cuts out for a beat, then says, "Hey, I have to go. There's another call coming in."

"Okay, cool. I'll talk to you later. Oh, and one more thing."

"Yeah?"

"Thanks, Addison. You're the best."

We disconnect, and since I don't see Arden's car yet, I sit and think about how I never thought I'd say, "Thanks," to my former nemesis.

Man, how things have changed.

Addison and I are pretty good friends now.

"Crazy," I mutter.

Even crazier is how there are times—and they're becoming more frequent—when I wonder what it'd be like if she and I explored more than friendship.

I mean, we're wildly attracted to each other. That hasn't changed. I see it in the way she looks at me when she thinks I'm not paying attention.

But I am.

I'm always tuned in to her.

And me?

Fuck, I definitely want her. She stars in my fantasies all the time.

But I'd never tell her that.

Yeah, even though I think she's feeling me, I don't want to ruin what we've built. It's better to leave things status quo.

We're in a good place.

Arden pulls in, and, needing to focus on something else, I jump out of my vehicle.

We meet up in the lot and head into the restaurant.

Once we're seated in a booth, Arden looks over at me curiously. "Dude," he says, "you look like you have a million things on your mind."

Guess my head's not cleared of Addison after all.

Still, I'm not about to share my romantic thoughts about her with Arden. He and Nils know we're getting along these days, and that's all they need to know. The friendship she and I have forged feels sacred or some shit.

So I just tell Arden about the magazine feature and act like that's what has me preoccupied.

"Whoa, damn." He lets out a low whistle. "That is fucking great, man."

"I know." I nod. "I think so too."

"And Addison landed it for you all on her own?"

I feel a sense of pride for her when I reply, "She sure as fuck did."

"Impressive."

The waiter comes around to drop off menus, and after he leaves, Arden, flipping his menu open, offhandedly says, "That Addison is some woman. Hot and smart. Fuck, maybe I should ask her out sometime."

Though I laugh and say, "Maybe," inside I'm bristling.

No, more like raging.

I feel like screaming, "Don't you fucking go anywhere near her!"

Or maybe I should just reach across the table and punch him in the face.

Wait, no.

He's my friend.

What is my problem?

He means nothing bad.

Addison and I aren't a couple.

We're merely friends and coworkers.

I have no claim over her.

I'm clearly overreacting.

Thank God Arden is engrossed in his menu and not paying a bit of attention to me, especially since I'm still glaring at him like a mofo.

Enough!

Opening my own menu, I stare down at it.

But it's nothing but a blur.

I'm far too distracted, trying to figure out what these strong feelings for Addison Knight might actually mean.

Shit, I don't think I want to know.

Chapter

Eighteen

ADDISON

Hayden does his interview with *Atlanta Sports Monthly*, and I get word, from him and the editor, that it goes extremely well.

When the magazine is released, in mid-December since it's a January issue, we should have a good feel on whether it's a success or not.

I have a feeling it'll be big.

But we have a couple more weeks to wait, including getting through Thanksgiving, which is today.

Speaking of the damn turkey holiday, I am freaking bored.

Hayden has been with the team all week for away games up in Canada. But the guys were supposed to get back late last night.

He asked me, via text, earlier this week if I was planning to go back to Pittsburgh to be with my family for the holiday.

I explained that, though I'd love to see my parents and sister, I'm too new to ask for enough time off from work to make the trip worthwhile.

He sent a sad-face emoji and texted, **Yeah, same here. We have away games the night after Thanksgiving and that Saturday afternoon, so no sense in traveling to Buffalo.**

He's lucky, though. I heard the team is putting on a nice spread of food down at the arena for all the guys who aren't from the US and those who are just staying in town.

I'm sure Hayden will be going and enjoying all that yummy goodness.

Me, I'll be eating turkey cold cuts for dinner.

Oh, yay.

I'm actually kind of hungry right now, as it's getting close to dinnertime.

Running my hands down my soft salmon-pink sweater and black leggings, I get up from the sofa and head to the kitchen.

Halfway there, the doorbell rings, scaring the crap out of me.

Jumping, and then detouring to the front door, I mutter, "Huh, who could be here? I'm not expecting any visitors."

Peering through the peephole, I'm shocked to see Hayden standing outside.

His chestnut hair is tousled, and he's wearing dark jeans and an untucked pale blue dress shirt. He's also holding two large brown paper bags, one in each hand, and he has what looks to be a magnum of champagne tucked in the crook of his arm.

Surprised but happy to see him, I swing open the door. "Hey."

"Hey, yourself," he says as he switches the bags to one hand and slides the champagne bottle down to his free one. Holding it up— *whoa, it's Dom Perignon*—he says, "Surprise! I hope you haven't eaten yet. I brought us Thanksgiving dinner and some bubbly to wash it down."

The savory aromas of the food waft up to my nose, and I am happier than ever that he's here.

"Wow, Hayden, this is awesome!" I bounce up and down on my pink-ballerina-flat-clad toes. "I am freaking starving," I confess. "In fact, I was just about to make a stupid cold sandwich. But this is so much better." I step aside. "Come on in."

He walks in, and we start toward the kitchen.

But I stop halfway there and turn to where he's following me.

His eyes fly up to my face, as if I didn't just catch him checking out my ass.

Funny, I don't mind a bit. I'm as guilty as he is, as I'm always sneaking in glances at him.

I wonder if he ever notices.

Acting as if I have no idea what he was up to, I get to why I stopped in the first place, asking, "This is a holiday, right?"

He lets out a relieved breath, then kind of peers at me curiously. "Yeah, it is. Why? What are you thinking?"

"Well…" I cross my arms. "Forget the kitchen. I think we should eat in the dining room." I gesture to the room next to where we're stopped. "You head in there now. Take the food out and put it on the table. While you're doing that, I'll go grab the nicer plates from the kitchen. Let's make this meal special."

"Sounds good to me," he says, chuckling. Then he reminds me, "Don't forget champagne flutes."

I give him a thumbs-up as I start to step away. "Don't worry, I'm on it."

A short while later, Hayden and I are seated across from each other at the dining room table, feasting on roasted turkey breast, herb-infused dressing, creamy whipped potatoes covered in a savory gravy, string beans, and cranberry sauce.

"Everything is so delicious," I remark as I dip my fork into my mashed potatoes. "Did you nab this food from the dinner the team hosted?"

"No." Hayden shakes his head as he cuts a piece off from the extra-large hunk of turkey breast on his plate. "I put in an order earlier this week, after you texted that you were sticking around town. I placed it with one of the nicer restaurants that was offering takeout today. I figured if we were stuck in town, we may as well enjoy a nice Thanksgiving dinner together."

"Mmm..." I spear a string bean. "This is nice. It's all delicious too. I really appreciate you sharing with me."

"Of course, Addison." His eyes meet mine. "There isn't anyone else I'd care to share Thanksgiving with this year."

Wow.

My heart skips a beat.

Looking away, I take a quick sip of champagne and ask him quietly, "Do you really mean that, Hayden?"

"Yeah, I really do."

Now my heart is pounding.

There's something happening here.

Holding up my flute, I share, "I feel the same way. So here's to what has turned into a really great friendship."

Our eyes meet again, and we both know this is turning into something more. That attraction we felt at the beginning, even when we hated each other, hasn't burned out.

No, it's ignited into something stronger, something that, one of these days, is sure to combust.

But for now, we do as we always do—we ignore it.

"Here, here." He reaches over the table and taps his glass to mine, averting his eyes. "I'll drink to that."

We each take a sip of champagne and then continue on with dinner, our growing attraction placed on the back burner…for now.

After we finish our tasty meal, Hayden unbuttons his sleeves and rolls them up his corded forearms. "I'm ready to help with the cleanup," he tells me.

Damn, I love a man who isn't afraid to pitch in with the boring stuff.

"Awesome." I stand and pick up the take-out container with what's left of the mashed potatoes. "Let's get started."

"You got it."

Together, we clear the table, placing the leftovers in the refrigerator and loading the dishwasher.

As Hayden hands me the last plate to put in, he remarks, "We make a good team, huh?"

"Yeah." I smile at him. "We do."

Closing the dishwasher, I turn it on.

With the cleanup completed, I run my hands down my leggings and ask, "So, what now?"

Cocking a brow, a move I once despised but am starting to adore, he says, "There's still quite a bit of champagne left. We could finish it off?"

Is this a good idea?

Catching a buzz and lowering our inhibitions?

Oh, hell, what's the worst that could happen?

I don't know, but a part of me really, really wants to find out.

So, smiling slyly, I say, "Let's do it."

Chapter

Nineteen

HAYDEN

The look Addison gives me when I suggest polishing off the bottle of champagne tells me everything I need to know—this fiery attraction between us is about to explode.

So be it, I say.

I'm tired of holding back and keeping my feelings for her in check.

And, fuck, it looks like she feels the same way.

Why else would she have just suggested playing a potentially dangerous game like Truth or Dare?

We're more than halfway through the Dom, and we're seated in her living room, our shoes kicked off and piled under the coffee table.

From my perch on the love seat, I look over at her on the sofa and level her with a mischievous grin. "Are you sure you want to play *that* game, sweetheart?"

"Huh." She taps her chin. "I think we're already playing, seeing as that sounds like dare number one. Like, do you dare me to play?"

"Okay, fair enough." I chuckle. "I'm obviously going first. Sooo… Do you accept that dare?"

She takes a sip of champagne, and, setting her flute down on the coffee table with a loud clink, she nods. "I sure as hell do, seeing as the game was my idea."

Laughing, I concede, "True."

We set some quick rules, which basically are that there are no rules.

Ahh, my favorite kind of game.

The only stipulation is that the game ends when someone refuses either the question or the dare. That person loses, and the other one wins.

"Simple enough." I jerk my chin to her. "You're up."

"All right." She leans back in the corner of the sofa, tucking a large throw pillow behind her back. "Truth or dare, Mr. Harrington?"

I think it over and go with "Truth."

She barks out a laugh. "Chicken."

"Ha ha. Just ask your question."

Laughing, she says, "Are you sure you're ready?"

"Yep."

"Okay, then. When was the last time you had sex?"

Surprised, as I wasn't expecting that inquiry, I blurt out, "Shit, woman. You get right to it, don't you?"

Shrugging, she says, "I guess I do. So are you going to answer the question or not?"

"I am." I sigh. "The answer is that it was a few months ago with Kristi."

"Really?" She seems shocked. "There's been no one since her? No puck bunnies on the road?"

I snort. "No. Contrary to popular belief, it's not like we have time for playing around on the road. I mean, maybe some teams do, but we keep a pretty tight schedule. On top of that, this is a good group of guys. Most of us are focused on hockey when we're traveling."

"That's good to know," Addison replies. "Apart from a hundred other potential problems, there are just too many diseases out there."

"There are," I agree somberly. "Not that I was ever as out of control as the rumors have portrayed me as being, but I've had my moments. In any case, I've been careful and lucky too. All of the teams I've played on have always required full physicals before the start of every season. That means taking every test imaginable. The good news is I know I'm clean and healthy in that regard."

"Yeah," she adds, "me too. I've never gone buck-wild crazy out there, either, but I've still always asked my doctor to run those kinds of tests. For the record—" Her eyes meet mine meaningfully. "—I'm good too."

Noted, I think but don't say out loud.

Come to think of it, I don't know why we're volunteering these kinds of facts. I mean, it's not like we're planning on sleeping with each other. Right?

Or are we?

Maybe we are, since we are divulging and so interested in such personal information.

Then again, it is Truth or Dare.

Yeah, it is.

That's why I ask, "What about you, Addison? When's the last time you got laid?"

Scrunching up her cute, pert little nose, she says, "Ugh, I hate that term. But in response to the question, it was last winter. I was dating a guy in Chicago for a few months. It obviously didn't work out, though."

"I'm sorry."

"No." She waves her hand. "It's no big deal."

An inexplicable wave of jealousy comes over me. And I'm totally not sorry. I hate that dude. I'm glad it was "no big deal," but, like when Arden said maybe he should ask Addison out, I hate the idea of another man touching her.

Why is that?

She's not mine.

But do you want her to be? a little voice inside my head asks.

Before I can censor myself, I blurt out, "Did you love him?"

Her eyes widen, and she responds, "No, I didn't. And that's two questions, buddy. Now I get to ask two in a row. Or"—she raises a brow—"you can choose two dares."

"Ha!" I laugh as I reach over to lift the bottle off the table.

Filling up my flute, I say, "If these questions are any indication of the type of dares that might come up, I think I'm going to need more champagne before we go *there*."

"Shit, you're not kidding." Leaning forward, she picks her glass up off the table and holds it out. "Fill me up, too, okay?"

"You got it."

With our champagne refreshed, we lean back into our respective spots. "Truth or dare?" she asks.

"Just truth for now. Like I said, I'm afraid to do two dares just yet."

Laughing, she says, "Okay." And then, without missing a beat, she fires out, "Have you ever been in love…and, if so, with whom?"

Yes, and maybe a little with you.

Shit, where did that come from?

Taking a big gulp of bubbly, I lower my flute and say, "I thought

I was in love once. But I was only eighteen. She was my high school sweetheart. I guess, for that time, I was. So, yeah, I'll say yes."

My head keeps telling me I know love feels differently from how I felt back then. My feelings for that girl in high school, though strong, weren't anything close to the way I feel about the woman across from me right now, who is currently peering over at me curiously.

I meet her gaze, and as she swallows hard, her greens telling me she feels something too.

Something strong, something intense.

Holy fuck, is Addison Knight falling for me as much as I'm falling for her?

Is this whole thing more than friendship, more than lust?

I ask her with my eyes, and she whispers, "Hayden…"

I'm about to say, "Babe, what's happening here?"

But just as I open my mouth, her expression turns mischievous, and she says, "You know what?"

"What?"

"I think it's time for some dares. Enough with the stalling. Let's be brave and adventurous."

Now when our eyes meet, there's a different kind of sparkle in hers.

Looks like shit's about to get dirty.

"Hell, yeah," I say.

As that is fine with me.

Chapter

Twenty

ADDISON

'm playing with fire, and I know it. But I don't care. Even though neither of us will openly admit it, Hayden and I are falling for each other.

I feel it.

I know it.

It just is what it is.

And maybe it's because the champagne has emboldened me, but I'm ready to take us to the next level.

That's why I say, "I think it's time for some dares. Enough with the stalling. Let's be brave and adventurous."

"Hell, yeah," he responds, a new kind of fire in his eyes.

Hayden gets to go first, as it's his turn.

I remind him of that, and he says, "I'll start with an easy one."

I shrug. "It's your choice."

He points to the champagne flute in my hand and throws out, "I dare you to chug the rest of that Dom."

Ha, wait until he hears my dare for him.

I snort. "That really is an easy one."

There's not much champagne left in my flute as it is, so chugging it down is a snap.

After I complete my dare, I tilt my empty flute at him and ask, "Still up for a dare for your turn?"

"Fuck," he scoffs. "Bring it on, babe."

Damn, I used to hate his terms of endearment, but now they make me feel all warm and tingly inside.

Actually, it is a little warm in the room.

And that inspires my dare.

Leaning forward, I set my empty flute on the coffee table, and, nodding to his chest, I say, "I dare you to take off your shirt."

His brows fly up. "Wait. Is this Truth or Dare or strip poker?"

"Ha ha." I roll my eyes. "Do you accept the dare or not?"

"What do you think?" he chuffs.

After setting his glass down on the table, he starts unbuttoning his shirt ever so slowly.

Kill me now.

I can't tear my gaze away as his smooth, hard chest is slowly revealed.

"Hmmm," I murmur, "looks like we have a 'yes' response."

Calling me out, as he knows me so well, he says, "It looks like you're enjoying it too."

Shrugging, I admit, "I am. It's not a bad view."

It's not. Hayden has an incredible body, all taut and tight.

I let out a long sigh, and, laughing, he takes his shirt all the way off, balls it up, and tosses it aside.

"Okay, your turn," he says. "Do you choose truth or dare?"

Taking a deep breath and preparing myself for absolutely anything, I exhale and state, "I'll take a dare."

"Brave girl."

"I know, right? So what do you got for me?"

He raises a brow. "Everything is on the table, right?"

"Absolutely everything," I confirm.

"All right, then." His eyes meet mine. "I dare you to take off your sweater."

This isn't too bad. At least I have on a cute black satin bra underneath. And I have matching panties…if we get to that point.

"Easy." I slide one arm out of my sweater before lifting it up and over my head. "Done."

When I look over at Hayden, his mouth is open a little, and his eyes are glued to my chest.

I look down.

Hmm, my breasts are kind of overflowing the cups. I guess it does look a bit Victoria's Secret-esque.

I clear my throat, and, swallowing hard, Hayden finally raises his gaze to meet mine.

"Cat got your tongue?" I ask, smirking.

"Something's got it," he murmurs.

That gives me an idea, but we'll have to work up to it.

"Truth or dare?" I ask.

He laughs. "Is there even an option at this point? Dare, of course."

"Can it be a two-parter? I mean, because the first part is really easy."

Looking confused, he asks, "And the second part isn't?"

Determined to keep it vague, I tell him, "I guess that's something only you can decide."

I know I have his interest piqued, so I'm not surprised when he goes for the two-part dare.

Sitting up straight, I then say, "Part one is I dare you to come sit next to me."

"No problem." Standing, he says, "This *is* an easy one."

"Right?" As he walks over to the sofa, I pat the spot next to me.

"That close?" he asks, staring down at my hand.

"Yeah." I nod. "You need to be that close to accept part two of the dare."

Shaking his head and chuckling, he sits down. "Okay, Addison." He turns to me, and we are so freaking close I can feel the heat emanating from him. It's making me dizzy with lust. "What is part two of this dare?"

Damn, his voice is so sexy up this close.

And I don't dare look down at his bare chest.

After taking one deep gulp of air, I finally whisper, "I dare you to kiss me."

Chapter

Twenty-One

HAYDEN

Whoa, *wait, what?*

Did I hear her right?

Did Addison Knight just ask me to kiss her?

And do so while we're seated on her sofa with our chests bare?

Well, she does have on a bra. But barely. Her breasts are spilling over the black satin cups, just begging me to free them, maybe take one in my mouth.

Fuck, maybe that'll be my next dare.

So what am I waiting for?

I scoot in closer, but she's not getting what she wants just yet. No, I'm going to make her really fucking want this kiss.

Leaning in, I skim my nose gently up along her soft, silky neck.

Sucking in a breath, she tilts her head to accommodate me.

I nibble and kiss and nip, then move to the other side, kissing up along her jawline, then whispering in her ear, "You know, I've dreamed about doing this."

She lets out a lusty groan and murmurs, "Hayden…"

"Yes?"

"Just don't stop."

"Oh, I don't plan to, babe. I haven't completed my dare yet, have I?"

"No," she gasps, arching up into me, making me hard, hard, *hard*.

Damn, I know she wants this kiss, and I'm ready to give it to her.

I trail my lips down along her cheek, and her eyes close.

Leaning back, I say, "Look at me, Addison."

Her eyes blink open, and I cup her face in my hands, holding her like she's fragile and might break.

I know she won't, but I want to cherish her, treasure her. She deserves nothing less.

As our gazes meet, there's lust in hers, as I'm sure there is in mine.

I lean forward, closing my eyes, and our lips touch.

We hold still, breaths commingling, taking in this moment that's been so long in coming.

There are words I want to say, but I talk instead with my mouth— kissing her ever so gently, then more urgently.

I think the game is over, and we both have won, as this is what victory feels like.

I let out a grunt, and she a groan, and I lay her down beneath me on the sofa.

There's a moment of levity when her hair gets stuck between her back and the throw pillow.

We stop, sharing a laugh.

I help her lift up, freeing her hair, and then we press back together, her chest to mine, her hands winding into my hair.

Ahhh, exquisite.

The only impediment to full skin-on-skin is her bra. Oh, and my jeans and her leggings.

I'll worry about all those later.

For now, I'm just enjoying her—kissing my way down to her collarbone, plumping her breasts in my hands, and laving my tongue between her two beautiful peaks.

I toy at the front closure of her bra, stopping just long enough to catch her gaze.

There's questioning in mine, and I do the one move I know used to drive her crazy. I think it still does—me cocking one brow—but in an entirely different kind of way.

She nods slightly, and, eyes holding hers, I snap open the pesky clasp.

I look down.

Her nipples are hard, and I am fucking on them in an instant, sucking one, then the other into my mouth greedily, like a man who's been starved.

In a way, I have. My hunger for her has grown steadily. And I need her so fucking much right now.

I want to devour this woman and have her in every kind of way.

So, as I suck and lick and nibble, and she writhes and moans, I tug at her leggings.

She rises and reaches down to help me.

Together, we wiggle her pants off, along with her sexy black satin panties that match her bra.

Rising up, I look down at her. "You're beautiful. You know that, right?"

She shakes her head, and I place a finger over her lips. "No, you are. Tell me."

"I'm beautiful?" she states softly.

It's more of a question, but that's okay.

I just tell her again, tracing my finger down along her body, between her breasts, until I'm holding one hip.

"What should I do to you first?" I ask, popping open the button on my jeans.

"I don't know," she murmurs, taking in the hard outline of my cock. "But I have an idea."

"No." I chuckle, shaking my head. "Not that."

"Why?" she asks.

Blowing out a breath, I confess, "I don't have a condom."

"You don't need one," she says. "Before I moved down here, I got a shot for birth control. I figured it would hold me over for six months until I found a doctor down here. Just in case, you know…" She smiles at up me. "I met someone."

Now I'm smiling back because there's nothing stopping us now. We already had that "other" conversation.

So we are fucking good to go.

But I want to take this slowly. My first night having Addison Knight is going to be something we both remember for all the right reasons.

Good thing I know just how to kick it off.

Reaching over to the coffee table, I pick up the bottle of Dom. There's not much left in it, but it's just enough.

Tipping the bottle ever so slightly above her body, a tiny bit of champagne trickles out and down between her breasts. It then runs down her stomach, and lower still.

There, perfect.

Placing the bottle back on the table, I lean down and glide my tongue along the path of champagne, moving lower, lower…

As I take her nub into my mouth, she gasps, "Hayden."

She is so fucking wet as I work her, my tongue on her clit, two fingers thrusting into her hot pussy.

She's groaning and moving, and the taste of skin and Dom and her sex is fucking making my cock about to burst out of my jeans.

But I go and go until she falls apart, coming so hard it even makes me dizzy.

"Damn," she says as I slowly kiss back up along her body.

"Feel good?" I murmur as I nuzzle her neck.

"Better than good," she breathes out.

Slowly, I rise up to my knees and start to unzip my jeans.

I guess I'm too slow, though, as Addison, huffing, commands, "Get those damn things off, Hayden. It's my turn to see all of you."

"Well, shit, woman, okay. You'll get no argument from me on that." I laugh and stand long enough to tug my jeans down and off.

I kick them aside, but as I start to lie back down with Addison, she stops me. "Uh-uh-uh," she tsks. "Those boxer briefs need to go too."

I ditch those in record speed. "Done."

When I kneel back down on the sofa, she wraps her silky-smooth legs around me, pulling me down to cover her body.

"I love feeling your weight on me," she says, wrapping her arms behind my neck.

As she writhes beneath me, creating friction between our skin-on-skin contact, leaving me damn near out of my mind with lust, I mutter, "It feels pretty fucking good to me too."

Our lips meet then, and our mouths open, tongues touching, dancing. She scoots down while I shift, my cock sliding along her wet pussy.

I gasp, and she groans, and the head of my dick pushes in ever so slightly. But I stay as still as I can, just savoring the moment.

When our mouths break apart, she begs me for more.

I can't hold off a second longer—I thrust up into her as far as I can.

"Fuuuccckkk…"

I go still again, and she does this time too.

"Oh my God, Hayden. This feels… I can't even say."

"I know."

Her eyes hold mine, and then I finally start to move, so slowly, so tenderly. There will be time for going wild later.

She closes her eyes, and I lean down, my lips on the side of her neck, kissing up along her jaw, making love to this woman I once hated.

Damn, isn't life crazy?

Chapter

Twenty-Two

ADDISON

I can't believe Hayden and I have become lovers. The man I once despised somehow first became my friend, and now that has blossomed into something more.

Is it love?

Biting my lip, I consider the possibility as I watch him sleep, the early morning light seeping in through the blinds.

We migrated up to my bed after the most amazing sex I've ever had in my life. It was just as mind-blowing the second time around when we woke in the middle of the night tangled up with each other, bare and skin-to-skin.

And now here we are.

But back to the question—are we in love?

I feel like we've been falling for each other for a while now. Last night was the culmination of that and our intense attraction.

But are we there yet—fully "in love"?

I'm not sure.

Neither of us dared to say the words last night, so maybe it's smart to just feel out this new direction in our relationship.

Yeah, let's see how things go.

Hayden starts to stir, and when he opens his eyes and sees that I'm awake, he pulls me in close to him. "Come here, you."

I nestle into his side, resting my chin on my arm on his chest so I can look up at him.

Reaching down to play with my hair, he says, "How do you feel today?"

"About what happened?"

He nods. "Yeah."

Hmm, here we go. We're clearly about to have the "where do we stand" talk.

Good, I want to know.

Tentatively, I tell him, "I feel good. What about you?"

"Fuck." He chuckles. "I feel amazing."

That makes me smile and feel reassured.

Still, I have to ask, "No regrets, then?"

Now he looks worried. "Of course not." He lifts his head up off the pillow to peer down at me. "What about you? Regrets?"

"Not a one," I share.

Flopping back down, he blows out what sounds like a relieved breath. "Good, good."

"So what happens now?" I just flat-out ask.

His hand stops in my hair, and he looks down at me again. "What do you want to happen, Addison?"

I'm just honest. "Well, I assume we're kind of seeing each other now, like romantically."

"I think that's clear," he agrees as he resumes toying with my hair.

"I don't have any desire to date anyone else."

"Good. Me neither."

We agree to take it slow, though, and just let things unfold.

Thinking about our work situation, I say, "Should we keep our relationship under wraps for now, seeing as we both work for the Thunder?"

Shrugging, he says, "I don't think it matters. There's no clause that states we can't date. At least there's nothing like that in my contract."

"Yeah, not in mine either. Still, if we put it out there that we're together, it could create a lot of pressure."

"You mean for us to succeed as a couple?"

"Yeah."

He thinks it over, then says, "Okay, that all makes sense. And since we're taking things slowly anyway, it's probably smart to keep our relationship to ourselves. Oh, but I may tell Arden. And probably Nils too."

Hmm, Nils was like an afterthought, but he sure had a funny look on his face when he mentioned Arden. It was clearly territorial.

I wonder if Arden expressed some kind of interest in me.

Aww, I think my guy is jealous.

In a weird way, that comforts me.

With our relationship status decided for now, we decide to get up, shower, and grab a quick breakfast.

Hayden downs his glass of orange juice while we're seated at my kitchen table, then he says, "Okay, so I'd love to spend the day with you, but our flight to Florida leaves in, like, a little over an hour. I need to go back over to my house, pack a bag, and get my ass to the airport."

"I know." I sigh. "I saw in the schedule that you play the Panthers tonight and the Lightning tomorrow afternoon. Is that right?"

"Yeah, it is," he confirms. "It's going to be hectic. But I'll be back tomorrow night if you want to hang out."

I smile. "Yeah, I'd like that."

We have plans already for as soon as he gets back?

Yes!

This relationship is definitely on.

Chapter

Twenty-Three

HAYDEN

On the flight down to Florida, I think a lot about Addison. I'm glad we had the "relationship" talk. It wasn't even stressful. Taking it slow is a great idea. I'm happy we both agree on that. Though my feelings for her are intense, I don't want us to rush into something and fuck things up.

But one thing I want to hurry up on is letting Arden know Addison is off-limits. It sucks that I can't tell him now, as he's seated right next to me on the team plane, but there are too many players within hearing distance.

And since we're keeping our relationship between us for now, I have to wait.

I like that we're keeping it quiet.

I want it to feel special.

Damn it, it *is* fucking special.

I've never known something could feel so fucking right.

I don't talk much on the flight. In fact, everyone is fairly quiet. I guess we're all just focused on tonight's game against the Panthers.

For me, though, Addison is also on my mind.

That woman just fucking owns me.

Even on the bus ride from the airport to the hotel the team is staying in, I feel the need to text her.

> **Me: We just arrived in Fort Lauderdale. I miss you, and I hope you're having a good day.**

> **Addison: Hmm, I feel very relaxed. Almost euphoric. I wonder why that is...**

She adds a little thinking person emoji, and I laugh.

> **Me: I'm happy you feel good, babe. But you just wait until tomorrow night. Euphoria is just the start.**

> **Addison: Damn, I can't wait.**

> **Me: Same, sweetheart.**

The bus reaches the hotel, and I wrap up with her.

Thankfully, the next few hours fly by.

I take a short nap, join the guys for a pregame snack, and then we all take a bus over to the arena.

The game with the Panthers turns out to be a tight defensive matchup. There's not much scoring, and we're still tied 1-1 by the start of the third period.

Things then start to open up.

Finn scores a goal at 11:02.

Then I set up Nils on a sweet two-on-one, and he buries the puck in the net.

We win the game 3-1.

Even though we have a very early flight over to Tampa for a late-afternoon game with the Lightning, by the time we make it back to the team hotel, Arden, Nils, and I are fucking starving. Most of our teammates are heading to bed, but we decide to grab a quick bite in the hotel restaurant.

It works out well, as we have a table to ourselves in a dark corner.

Good, we can talk without being overheard. I really want to let the guys know I'm seeing Addison now—especially Arden—but I'm waiting for the subject to come up.

So far, it's been all hockey talk.

But then Arden, setting his fork down and pushing away his mostly empty plate of pasta, asks, "So, are you and Addison still getting along okay?"

Cryptically, just to keep them wondering before I divulge the sure-to-be-surprising update, I reply, "Er, uh…you could say that."

I smirk, and Nils looks over at me curiously.

Chuckling, he says, "You hooked up with her, didn't you?"

All I have to do is laugh, and they know.

Arden shakes his head. "I knew it was going to happen. All that hate from early on had to come out somewhere. I suspected it was always fueled by lust."

I take a sip of water, then set the glass down. "Yeah, it was. But now it's more than that."

"Whoa." Arden looks surprised. "So it's going to be more than a onetime thing."

"Definitely." I nod. "For sure."

Nils smiles. "Hey, I'm happy for you. I hope it all works out."

"Yeah, me too," Arden adds.

I can see they're both sincere and their sentiments are genuine. It makes me feel good that I have these two guys as friends.

Feeling like I can talk straightforward with them, I reveal that we're going to take it slowly and see how things go.

"We want to keep our relationship on the down-low for now," I further explain. "You guys are the only two I'm saying anything to. That's the plan, for now."

"I hear ya," Arden says. "I think that's smart. And don't worry. We won't say a word to anyone."

"Yeah," Nils agrees. "It's your and her prerogative to let the world know when the time is right."

"Thanks, guys," I say. "Still, keeping it quiet is going to suck a little, seeing as I'd like to take Addison out on some proper dates. I don't want us to be seen and photographed, though. Then the whole hockey world will know immediately."

Nils, leaning back in his chair, says, "What about going to a local park, maybe just taking a nice walk? I hear Sunday's going to be mild and sunny back up in Atlanta."

I nod, thinking it over. "That's not a bad idea. But the public parks always get so crowded on good weather days, especially this time of year."

Arden seems to consider something, and then he says, "You can always take a hike up at my place. I own about half the woods, making it all private property. There are a bunch of cool nature trails back behind my house that are perfect for walking or hiking. Best part is I guarantee you'll have those trails all to yourselves."

Arden is a good guy, and now that he knows Addison and I are seeing each other and she's off-limits, I don't have to worry about him making any moves on her.

Nodding, I say, "That sounds perfect. I have to run it by Addison, but I'm sure she'll love the idea."

"Just come up on Sunday anytime," Arden tells me. "I'll leave the front gate to my property open. If I'm not around, park in the driveway and head to the back of the house. You can't miss the trailheads."

"Thanks, man."

"No problem. In fact, take a look around the whole area. The property adjacent to mine is for sale. You may want to think about building a house up there. It's not as close to the arena as where you're living right now, but like we talked about once before, the longer commute isn't a bad trade-off for all that solitude and beauty. I gripe about it now and then, but I truly wouldn't change a thing."

"Hey, I hear you," I reply. "Solitude and beauty are what I'm looking for these days."

It's true. There was a time I once craved being where the action was. But as I've grown as a person, I see things differently.

If Addison and I do take that hike behind Arden's property, I want to hear her thoughts on the idea of building a house out there.

Her input and opinions are really important to me.

Why is that, Hayden?

I know the answer, though I'm not ready to say it out loud.

I can keep it quiet all I want, but the fact is I've fallen in love with Addison Knight.

Chapter

Twenty-Four

ADDISON

The Thunder win their away game against the Panthers on Friday night and also the one against the Lightning on Saturday. Hayden actually scores the game-winning goal in that one.

The game is over by about six, but he doesn't get back to Atlanta till late. He walks in his door around midnight, and, since I heard his car driving up, I'm waiting for him in the entry hall.

"Babe…" He wraps me in a warm hug. "I missed you."

"I missed you too," I murmur.

Stepping back and looking down at me, he cups my face, so gently, so sweetly.

We smile at each other, then he leans down to kiss each of my cheeks, the tip of my nose, and then his lips find my mouth.

I kiss him back, melting to putty in his strong, capable hands.

Oh, how I love those hands, especially the way they slide down my back and grab my ass.

After a quick squeeze, Hayden pulls back just enough to say gruffly, "I want you in my bed right fucking now."

I jump up in his arms, his hands back on my ass as I wrap my legs around him. "Let's go," I say.

He kicks off his dress shoes, then his mouth is on mine the whole way up the stairs and down the hall to his bedroom.

Together, we collapse onto his bed—laughing, kissing, touching.

He tugs off my jeans and socks, his slacks, and my long-sleeve mint-green top. Then his taupe button-down shirt is tossed aside, along with his socks.

We're all over each other then, pushing the comforter aside as I roll on top of him.

With my hair framing my face, I peer down at my man.

Damn, he's so muscular and toned. "You have, like, a perfect body," I say, running my hand down his hard chest and over his taut abs.

He chuckles. "Thanks, babe."

My hand trails lower till I'm grasping and stroking his cock.

Letting out a gasp, he closes his eyes and lets me have my fun.

"You played so well," I say as I scoot down and lower my head to where my hand is sliding up and down along his hard, throbbing shaft. "I think you deserve a reward."

He doesn't have time to answer as I take him in my mouth, licking and working him.

Lowering his hand into my hair, he groans, "Yeah, like that. Fuck."

As I glide my tongue along the underside of his throbbing cock, I peer up at him from under my lashes.

Opening his eyes, he looks down and mutters, "Shit, Addison, if you keep that up, I'm going to come." Sitting up, he scoots back so his cock pops out of my mouth. "Come here, beautiful."

He beckons me to him, and I crawl into his lap, so wet and ready that I only need to lift up to slide down onto what I really, really want.

So I do, eliciting from him a "Damn, woman."

"I need you like this," I whisper as I rise up and down, milking his cock with my pussy. My eyes flutter shut as I swallow hard and add, "Let me play."

Hayden has no reservations about that, not that I thought he would. He loves every minute of me fucking him.

I go fast.

I go slow.

I work us in ways that build me up to a crescendo, like a wave that's about to come crashing down.

When I do tumble, Hayden comes with me.

We hold on to each other, and with my head tucked in his neck, I mouth words he can't hear but ones I feel in the depths of my being, "I love you."

The next day, we drive up to Arden's house to take a hike in the woods. I was more than up for the idea when Hayden ran it by me.

And here we are.

Since it's so mild out, we've opted for jeans, flannel shirts over long-sleeve tees, hiking boots, and light jackets.

"Wow, it's really beautiful up here," I remark as we step out of Hayden's Cayenne. "All these woods remind me of home."

"Yeah, same here," he says as he closes the SUV door and walks over to me. "I bet it's really pretty up here in the summer."

All the trees are bare since it's late November, but it's easy to imagine how lush and green they'll all look in a few months.

Hayden takes my hand, and we meander along a stone walkway that leads to the back of Arden's very large home. It's easy to pick out the trailheads even from across his expansive lawn.

We choose a wide dirt path that appears to head deeper into the surrounding forest, and then we start out on our way, hands joined as we walk side by side.

As we traverse the flat but winding terrain, there are parts where we must go single file.

I take the back and let Hayden lead, solely so I can check out his ass, which looks fantastic in his jeans.

I don't think he even catches on to my wily ways.

Then again, maybe he does, seeing as he just looked back for a beat and caught me red-handed.

He turns back and laughs, and I ask innocently, "What?"

"Like I didn't just catch you checking out my ass," he throws out over his shoulder.

The trail widens, and I scamper back up next to him.

"Okay, I'm busted," I admit. Reaching over to grab his firm ass, I give him a light squeeze. "It's so nice. I just couldn't help myself."

That makes him laugh again, and I realize I love the sound of him being happy.

It makes me smile too.

"Aw, babe, that's fine with me. But..." His eyes sparkle mischievously. "I get to walk behind you next. Fair is fair, right?"

"Right," I agree. "We have a deal."

We're quiet for a while, until we reach a line of wooden poles with pink plastic ribbons tied on to them.

Stopping, Hayden says, "This must be the end of Arden's property."

"Should we turn back around?" I ask.

"Nah." He shakes his head. "I actually want to check out this area a little more. Arden said this land is for sale."

Whoa, wow, this is news.

Surprised, I ask, "Are you thinking about buying and building up here?"

"I am," he confirms with a nod. "But I'd like your opinion first."

I blink at him, touched. "You would?"

"Yes." He takes my hand. "It's important to me what you think before I make any final decisions."

My heart flutters. Hayden wouldn't be asking for my opinion on things, like where he may build a freaking house, if he didn't see a future with us.

Squeezing his hand, my whole being filled with joy, I tell him, "Let's go check it out, and I'll be sure to share my every thought."

Chapter

Twenty-Five

HAYDEN

I need to tell Addison something, and I need to do it soon. I need to tell her that I fucking love her.

Yeah, there's no more wondering about it.

I love the woman.

That is a fact.

I've known it for a while now, but I became 100 percent sure the other day when we were hiking out on Arden's property and beyond.

It became clear when we checked out the property for sale next to his—the woods all around and the huge field in the middle, where an equally huge house could be built. When my whole decision was dependent on if Addison liked the area or not, that's when I knew.

And, as it turns out, she loves the property.

So I put a bid on it earlier this week, the day after our hike. I haven't heard anything yet, but we'll see where and how it goes from here.

Right now, though, I have a game to focus on. We're about to take the ice in Chicago for our matchup tonight with my former team, the Blackhawks.

To say it's important for me to play well is an understatement.

Yeah, I have something to prove.

Even though it worked out better for me in every way, shape, and form that I'm with the Thunder, I'm still burned that the Blackhawks traded me.

Talk about a fucking insult.

"Time for a little payback," I murmur as our team is announced and we skate out onto the ice to a chorus of boos.

That's not surprising, as we are the away team.

On the bench, Coach reminds us to stick with our game plan and we'll have success.

He's right—by the end of the first period we're up 4-2. This isn't our usual tight defensive style of play; both teams are opening up tonight.

But that's okay. We're still playing our game our way.

In the second period, we score another goal, but so do the Hawks.

Later, with seven minutes and ten seconds left in the third period, a former teammate of mine checks me hard into the boards.

"What the fuck?" I yell.

He just laughs and turns his back.

Not so fast, pal.

Pissed, I skate over and cross-check him.

Annnnd I get caught.

I don't even try to argue the penalty; I just head to the sin bin and take a seat.

It sucks that I just put our team at a disadvantage. But our penalty kill is pretty good. Let's hope they keep the Blackhawks from scoring.

I watch as our guys do a stellar job of clearing the pucks up ice a number of times. The Hawks can't seem to even get set up.

Good.

Time ticks down, and I stand when there are only a few seconds left of my penalty.

4...3...2...1...

The door opens, and I skate out of the box just as Nils is clearing the puck.

Fortuitously, it lands right on my stick.

Yes!

I'm on a breakaway and skate as quickly as I can into the opponent's zone.

I'm fast, so within seconds, it's just me and the goaltender.

I know this guy and all his moves from when we were teammates.

He likes to go low.

So I go high, shooting the puck up above his left shoulder.

It goes in.

Goal!

The crowd boos, but my teammates on the ice converge around me, hugging me and patting me on my helmet.

I'm thrilled that I made up for my penalty by scoring a goal.

The rest of the game goes by quickly, and we end up winning by a score of 6-3.

In the locker room, the mood is jovial. There's a lot of joking around and laughing. I love when it's like this.

I shower and slip on the same navy pinstripe suit I wore to the game. I'm ready before a lot of the guys are showered and dressed. That's okay, as there's a little time till we have to board the bus to head to the airport and fly to our next stop—Columbus—for one more away game tomorrow.

I can't wait to get back to Addison. She's all I can think about. Texting, FaceTiming, and talking on the phone, those things just aren't enough. I want to see her, and hold her, and love her like only I can do.

Soon, I tell myself.

We already made plans for her to be at my house when I fly back tomorrow after the game. It'll be late, but I want her in my bed and ready for me when I get home.

The things I plan to do to her...

While I'm daydreaming about my girl, one of our trainers, Rob, a middle-aged guy who's been in hockey forever, comes over to me. "Hey, Harrington, someone outside the locker room wants to see you."

Huh?

"Who is it?" I ask.

He shrugs. "I don't know. Just some girl."

Okay, this is weird. It can't be a fan, as not just anyone can waltz around the locker room area.

Maybe it's a reporter.

Standing up from the bench I'm seated on, I head out into the hall.

I look around but don't see anyone.

But then I catch sight of a girl with a long blonde ponytail, wearing jeans, tall black boots, and a baby blue faux fur jacket. She's leaning against the wall a bit down from me, right where the arena curves.

"Kristi?" I blurt, stunned.

"Hey, Hayden." Pushing off the wall, she walks over to where I'm standing. "Can we talk for a minute?"

"Um, I guess, sure." I gesture to the wall she was leaning against.

"Let's go back over there. It'll be more private."

She nods. "Okay."

I don't know what this chick wants from me, but I'll give her a few minutes. I have time to kill right now anyway. Maybe she wants some sort of closure. Despite her knifing me in the back, I'm willing to at least give her that.

Once we're a good ways away from the locker room, even farther down from where she was originally standing, she leans back against the wall like she was doing before.

"So," she begins, reaching out with the toe of her boot to touch the tip of my left dress shoe. "How have you been?"

I take a step back.

I'm not here for small talk or to play footsie.

Ignoring her question, I ask dryly, "Kristi, what do you want?"

"Okay, fine," she huffs. "Play it that way."

I blow out a breath. "Look, I'm not playing anything. I'm done with games. I'm actually seeing someone now, so if you can just tell me why you called me out here, that'd be great."

I'm not about to tell her who I'm dating. That's Addison's decision on when, or if, she wants Kristi to know. Not to mention, we're still keeping our relationship quiet. This chick would shout it from the rooftops just to be the first to announce it to the hockey world.

Rolling her big brown eyes at me, she grumbles, "Wow, you're not much fun anymore, are you?"

"Kristi, I'm losing patience."

I'm about to turn around and head back into the locker room, but then she says something I thought I'd never hear. "Look, Hayden, I'm sorry. I just wanted to tell you that in person. That's why I wanted to see you. I hope you and whoever you're dating are happy."

"We are," I confirm. "And thank you for apologizing."

It doesn't change the situation, but it's nice to know she has some sense of remorse.

Softly, she murmurs, "I wish things had worked out differently for us."

I remind her, "That was never in the cards, not for us. It was just a short, fun time. You knew that. I never made any promises, and you told me you were cool with casual."

"I know," she confesses, pushing away from the wall. "And I was. But then I guess I wasn't. Hey, a girl can dream, right?"

I don't even know how to respond to that, and I'm sure it shows.

Scoffing, she says, "It doesn't matter, not anymore. I'm seeing someone too."

"That's good, Kristi. I'm glad for you. Anyway..." I glance toward the locker room. "I better get back in there."

She sighs. "Okay. But before you go, can I ask you for a favor?"

I'm reticent, but concede, "Um, okay."

"Can I have a hug, Hayden?"

"Oh, Kristi, I don't know."

"Just a little one," she pleads. "Like a final goodbye."

Ah, hell, I did say to myself that I'd give her some closure. I guess this is her way of saying farewell.

So, reluctantly, I lean forward and give her a loose hug, patting her on the back.

"Okay, then." I step back and turn to walk away. "Bye."

As I spin around and stride off, I hear her, in a tone filled with a weird satisfaction and a sarcastic bent, mumble, "See you around, Hayden."

Fuck, did I just make a mistake by hugging her?

I think she read more into that than I intended.

Typical Kristi—seeing possibility that isn't there.

Hayden

Should I even tell Addison I saw her?
I was planning to, but now I don't know.
Maybe I'll just wait until I get back to Atlanta.
Then I can tell Addison everything in person.

Chapter

Twenty-Six

ADDISON

While Hayden is away with the team for games against the Blackhawks and the Blue Jackets, I concentrate on work.

The days fly by quickly, and the next thing I know, it's Friday.

Yay!

But before I leave the office, Ms. Garcia calls me in to inform me that, starting next week, I'll be working with more players.

Surprised, I ask, "What about me working exclusively with Hayden Harrington?"

She waves her hand. "You'll still be going with him to events, but most of those outings will now be with his teammates as well."

"Whoa, that's a change."

"It is." She nods. "But the current arrangement was never supposed to last forever, remember?"

"Yes." I nod.

She goes on, "Management is quite pleased with how Mr. Harrington has conducted himself in Atlanta. They're very happy with the work you've done with him. We're already hearing good feedback about that magazine feature you set up, and the issue isn't even out yet. Now management would like to see you apply that same skill set to the team as a whole."

Once I take all that in, I reply, "Wow, then I guess this is actually great news."

"It is, Addison." Ms. Garcia smiles. "This gives you more room to grow in your role as a consultant."

I was more referring to the fact that Hayden is no longer under the microscope, but I don't elaborate. He's going to be so pleased. I can't wait to talk to him. And maybe now that I'm not assigned to him exclusively one-on-one, we can start to think about revealing our relationship.

It's going so damn well. It seems like a million years ago that we were always at each other's throats.

This is *so* much better.

Before I leave work, I receive a text from Hayden to confirm that we're still on for late tonight after he gets back to Atlanta. The plan is for me to sleep over at his place, and though he'll be coming in late, he'll be coming in an entirely different way—*ha ha*—once he gets in bed with me.

I will be too.

And I can't freaking wait!

With a big smile plastered on my face, I text back that I will definitely see him later tonight. I don't mention anything about me now working with other players. I want to tell him that good news in person.

He's going to be beyond thrilled that all his hard work off the ice has paid off. Mine has too. The Thunder trust and love him.

And really, so do I, though in a much deeper, more profound way.

Yep, I love Hayden Harrington.

Maybe I'll even tell him that tonight.

And maybe he'll say it back.

I mean, I *think* he loves me.

It feels that way.

But we'll see.

Damn it, I just want him to say it out loud.

Tossing my phone in my bag and letting out a frustrated groan, I leave my office and head home.

A few hours later, after heating up leftovers for dinner and taking a long, hot shower that leaves me feeling quite relaxed, I pack a small overnight bag in my bedroom and then get ready to head next door to Hayden's house.

We exchanged alarm codes and backup spare keys a few weeks ago. That was when we were still just friends. It seemed like the prudent thing to do after my deck incident.

Of course, directly after that night, we never would have done that. But oh, how times have changed.

Shaking my head and smiling as I zip up my bag, my cell starts ringing.

It can't be Hayden, as the game against Columbus, which I plan to watch over at his house, is just about to begin.

As I grab my cell from where it's lying on my bed, I flip it around so I can see the screen.

Wow, it's Kristi.

Curious as to why she's getting back in touch with me after so many unreturned calls and texts on my part, I answer rather flippantly, "Hey. It's been a minute, huh?"

Sounding contrite—but with her, you never know—she says, "Aw, Addison, I'm sorry. I know I missed a bunch of your calls."

"And texts," I toss out.

"Yeah, those too. I planned on getting back to you, I really did. But I've just been *so* busy with my boyfriend."

Though she can't see me, I roll my eyes. "Would that still be the guy from the team?"

"Yes."

I don't even bother asking which player he is. I really don't want to know. She doesn't volunteer the info either.

What she does say is "Guess who I ran into last night in Chicago?"

Hmm, last night was the Thunder's game against the Blackhawks.

Carefully, I ask, "Um, who?"

Smugly, she replies, "I saw Hayden Harrington, in the flesh and in person. Can you believe it?"

Hmm, I don't like the sound of this.

My heart rate quickens, and I have to wonder why Hayden hasn't mentioned this to me. It seems rather pertinent, as he did have his dick in the girl. I'd like to know when he "runs into" her, especially "in the flesh and in person."

"Oh, really?" I reply slowly. "And just where did you see him?"

"Down by the locker rooms. We had a really nice talk."

My blood starts to boil as I snap, "You did, did you?"

What would my boyfriend have to talk about with her?

And why would he be conversing with her in the first place?

Unless…

Confirming all the ugly thoughts running through my mind, Kristi says, "He was very flirtatious, Addison. I think he wanted to hook up. You know, for old time's sake. Too bad for him I'm seeing someone. Still, he gave me a big-ass hug that felt wonderful."

What?

I'm angry.

I'm hurt.

Kristi has no idea that Hayden and I are together, so this is all on him.

Clenching my teeth, I grind out, "He gave you a *hug*?"

"Yep," she says on a sigh. "And let me tell you, the chemistry is still there. I felt it. Maybe I should have strayed. Hayden was always so amazing in the sack."

She has no idea I'm furious. But truly, if I could crawl through the phone and smack this bitch, I would.

Obviously, I can't do that.

I can get rid of her, though.

Still seeing red, I tell her, "I have to go. I think there's someone at my door."

"Oh, okay," she says, sounding confused. "I guess we'll just talk anoth—"

I hang up on her.

And then I throw the phone across the bed.

I am fucking fuming at Hayden.

Why didn't he tell me he saw Kristi and talked to her?

Oh, and hugged her.

We've talked and texted since then.

Hell, we even FaceTimed early this morning before I went to work.

I can think of only one reason why he'd stay quiet—he didn't want me to know.

And no wonder!

The jerk was flirting with Kristi, *hugging* her.

I was just thinking about how much I trust him.

And that I *love* him.

Ugh!

I am so stupid.

Hayden absolutely cannot be trusted.

I guess once a player, always a player. And I don't mean on the ice.

Bastard!

I should have known better.

And now I feel like such a fool.

Chapter

Twenty-Seven

HAYDEN

After we land in Atlanta, I race to get home. Home is where I'll find Addison in my bed. I plan to wake her with kisses and love up on her all night long.

More importantly, I'm going to bare my soul and share with her that I love her.

Fuck, man, I do.

After I pull into my garage, I don't even bother grabbing my bag from the back. I just get my ass upstairs as quickly as I can.

But, wait, this is weird.

There's no Addison in my bed.

I check back downstairs to see if maybe she fell asleep on the sofa while watching the game. She told me she planned to see it over here.

But no, she's not in the living room either.

This is strange.

It's late, like after two in the morning.

Should I text her?

I think about it and decide to give it a try. Though it seems to me that if she changed her mind about coming over, she would have let me know.

Shit, I hope everything is okay.

Quickly, I whip out my phone and text her.

Me: Babe, I'm home. Where are you? I thought you'd be in my bed, I'm sad that you're not. I was totally planning to make it worth your while.

I wait and wait, but she sends no reply.

Maybe she fell asleep over at her house?

That could easily have happened since our plans were for so late at night.

I finally decide that maybe this is better. The travel and games are catching up to me, and I'm feeling pretty wiped out.

I'll just crash and call Addison in the morning. It's Sunday, and there are no practices or morning skates.

It'll be nice to spend the whole day with her.

I don't wake up until after ten the next morning. The good thing is I feel completely refreshed.

I shower and dress in faded jeans and a black-and-silver Thunder hoodie, then I go downstairs to the kitchen, where I grab an energy bar and a glass of orange juice.

I devour the bar and down the juice in record speed.

Yeah, I'm a man with places to go, like over to Addison's house.

After slipping on socks and running shoes, I head next door.

Addison never replied to my text. I thought she'd get back to me this morning, but she could still be in bed.

Once I reach her front door, I ring the buzzer.

And then I wait…and wait…and wait.

Okay, now I'm starting to worry.

I hate to key in the code and just let myself in, as I don't want to startle or frighten her.

But, God, what if something happened?

She did lock herself out on the deck that one time.

I ring the doorbell once more, and then I start knocking frantically. "Addison, babe, are you in there? Are you okay?"

Crickets.

That's it—I'm going in.

But just as I'm keying in the code, the door swings open.

Startled, but relieved to see she's fine, I step back and say, "Hey."

Addison does not look happy. She does look cute, though. She's wearing a big bulky gray sweatshirt and distressed jeans, and her hair is up in a high ponytail.

"What's wrong?" I ask. "I thought we had plans last night, sweetheart. Did something happen?"

Snorting, she crosses her arms. "Ha, did something happen, huh? You could say so, Hayden. But of course, you'd know more about that than I do."

My brow furrows. "What does that even mean? And, by the way, can we talk about this inside? It's a little chilly out here this morning."

I don't know why she hasn't invited me in yet, but it looks like she's not going to.

Sure enough, she states, "We're fine just where we are, thank you very much."

Why is she being so weird and cryptic?

"All right." I grow serious. "Addison, for real, what's wrong?"

"Oh, let me see..." She starts tapping her sneakered foot. "Let's start with this—I received an interesting call last night."

Now I'm even more confused. "You did?"

"Yes, I sure the fuck did." She's glaring at me now. "It was my ole pal Kristi calling. She had some rather interesting updates, ones I hadn't heard before—from you or anyone. But mostly not from you, Hayden."

I let out a groan, to which she arches a brow.

Fuck, it all makes sense now—why Addison blew me off last night, why she didn't return my text, and why she looks ready to kill me at this very moment.

"Look," I begin, blowing out a breath. "I don't know what that crazy girl told you, but I can explain everything. You know she misreads shit. Regardless, I was planning to tell you all the details once I saw you in person."

"Well," she scoffs, "you're seeing me now, and it took me bringing it up to you for it to even come to your mind. You saw Kristi, and we talked after that. You never mentioned one word to me. Were you really going to ever say anything?"

"I was," I insist. "I told you I wanted to talk to you about it in person."

"I bet." She crosses her arms. "Why did you even talk to her, Hayden? She said you were flirting with her. She said she felt like you still wanted her."

"That's a fucking lie!" I shout. "She asked to see me. I was in the locker room, and one of our trainers came in and told me someone wanted to talk to me out in the hall. I had no idea who it was, but when I went out, I saw it was Kristi. I only spoke with her to give her some sense of closure or whatever. She actually apologized too. But, Addison, I swear to you that I did not flirt with her. Why would I?"

Narrowing her pretty green eyes at me, she snaps, "I don't know. But tell me one thing, Hayden."

"Sure, anything. What?"

"Did you hug her?"

Blowing out a breath, I confess, "Yeah, I did. But she asked me to, and it didn't mean—"

Holding up her hand, she cuts me off. "Stop. I don't want to hear another word. But I will say this, buddy."

"Yes?"

"We are fucking done."

"Wait, what?" I'm taken aback, so much so that I actually take a step back. "You're kidding me, right?"

"No." She shakes her head. "I'm serious. I'm not playing games like this with you. I just think it's better if we go back to a professional relationship. This, us"—she waves her hand between our bodies—"was clearly all a mistake."

Swallowing hard, I say softly, "You don't mean that."

"I do."

"Babe…"

Biting her lip and looking like she's about to cry, she chokes out, "Please, Hayden, just leave. I want to be left alone. Please."

I don't want to go.

I want to fix this.

But I have to respect her wishes as well.

Still, I'm not giving up on her.

She just needs some time.

"Okay." I start to go, but then I turn back. "Addison, there's one more thing I have to say."

"Make it quick," she snaps.

"Okay. I promise I'm going to fix this. And the reason why is because I lo—"

Bam!

She slams the fucking door in my face.

But before I walk away, even though she can't hear me, I finish my sentence. "I love you."

Chapter

Twenty-Eight

ADDISON

A s soon as I slam the door, I lean back against it and burst into tears. I don't know what Hayden was about to say, but I had to cut him off. If I hadn't, I might've given in.

Such a big part of me wants to talk it over and work things out simply because I love the jerk.

But I won't be made a fool.

I have too much self-respect.

And maybe a little too much pride, a little voice inside my head chirps.

Traitor!

But what if his version is the truth?

Do I really trust Kristi and what she told me?

Damn it, I don't know who to believe anymore.

That's why, at the very least, I need some time to process everything.

Over the next week, I do a good job of avoiding Hayden. I don't even look over at his house. And at work, there are no immediate events scheduled with him or any of the guys. That means I'm safe from having to interact with him.

That's something to be thankful for.

There hasn't been much else lately.

One positive thing, though, is the *Atlanta Sports Monthly* edition featuring Hayden came out.

And the response has been amazing.

Friday, in my office, I field a bunch of calls requesting interviews and offering opportunities for more features with Hayden. There are so many that I can't accept them all.

So I choose the most well-known outlets where he'll get the most exposure.

I hate doing anything nice for him when I'm so angry with the man, but it is my job.

Do I really feel that way, though?

Do I hate Hayden?

I'm coming to grips with the fact that I don't. I mean, hell, even a part of me is happy for him that the magazine feature is yielding great results.

But I don't *want* to be happy for him.

Too bad I can't help it.

I guess I'm not as strong as I thought I was.

The sad fact is I miss the guy like crazy.

I miss talking with him.

I miss having fun with him.

I miss joking around.

I just miss spending time together.

I also miss his body, and the things he does to me with it.

And I miss doing things to him.

I miss lying around with him afterward, feeling contented.

Okay, clearly I just miss everything about Hayden fucking Harrington.

He's part of my life now.

Or he was.

But mad or not, my heart still wants him.

Ugh, I hate love.

Why must it be so hard?

Sighing, I check the time and see it's almost five o'clock. I'll be leaving the office soon.

There's nothing else that really needs to be done, so I sit at my desk a while longer, just thinking about Hayden some more.

At one point, Ms. Garcia pops her head in and tells me, "Have a good weekend, Addison. See you on Monday."

"Thanks. You have a good one too." I give her a sad little wave. "Bye."

I don't know why I'm stalling on leaving. I guess it's because I'm not looking forward to a long, lonely weekend.

I wonder what Hayden is doing.

He had a home game last night, which the team lost. That sucks, but you can't win them all. The next matchup is also a home game, on Monday evening.

Hayden will probably be hanging around his house all weekend, much like I'll be doing next door.

Too bad we're over and done. We could have had a great time

together.

This is all so silly, that traitorous voice in my head snips with a huff. *You still could have a great time. Fix this!*

I almost cave.

Picking up my phone, I stare at the screen.

What to do, what to do?

A part of me wants to send Hayden a text. Doing so has been such a part of my daily routine for months. All week it's felt weird not communicating with him in some way.

Today, though, has been particularly hard.

I don't know why.

Just text him, the voice in my head says.

But what would I even say?

Tell him you forgive him. You know his account of that night is the truth, not Kristi's.

Do I, though?

I think if he had told me he loved me at some point—that is, if he even does—I'd feel more secure.

Hey, you never said it either.

No, no, I didn't.

And now it feels like it's too late.

Blowing out a breath and tossing my phone into my purse, I stand, readying to just freaking leave.

Nothing is going to be resolved—not today and maybe not ever.

Chapter

Twenty-Nine

HAYDEN

As the week after our fight wears on, I fully expect to hear something from Addison. I know it won't be regarding an event, as there are none this week. I've also been informed that Addison is no longer assigned to me exclusively.

That's actually a good thing.

It means we did it!

We successfully rehabilitated my image.

You'd think she'd contact me to celebrate our victory, right?

I mean, no one can be this stubborn.

Wrong!

Addison Knight can obviously be stubborn as a bull, as there's absolutely nothing from her all week—no calls, no texts, no let's-call-a-truce communication, nothing.

This is ridiculous.

By Friday, I'm actually pissed at her. She wouldn't even hear me out or give me the benefit of the doubt.

I attend our morning practice and even give a couple of reporters a quick interview in the locker room about how well the team has been playing. I then take a shower and dress in jeans and a tan button-down shirt.

Arden is busy with an interview of his own, so I don't have a chance to say, "See ya," or talk with him.

A part of me wants to get his opinion on if he thinks Addison is being unreasonable.

I've kept our big argument to myself all week. And it looks like it'll stay that way a while longer.

I'll have to fill Arden in on the events of my personal life another day.

I push Addison from my mind as I start back to my house. But then I get a call from the real estate agent informing me that the land next to Arden's property is mine.

There are a few papers to sign, but otherwise, it's a done deal.

Wow, I'm pumped.

I can start thinking about having my house built.

But my enthusiasm wanes quickly, as I was supposed to share this good news with Addison.

Now I'm more irritated than ever with that woman.

My blood starts to boil on the drive, and I'm fuming by the time I reach my house.

As I'm pulling into the garage, I notice a package lying on my walkway.

Huh, I didn't order anything.

After parking, I head back outside instead of going into the house.

As the garage door trundles down behind me, I stride over to the package.

Picking it up and turning it over, I find it's addressed to Addison.

"Oh, this is so fucking perfect," I mutter.

It really is, as I have a few things to say to her. And now an opportunity to do exactly that has fallen into my lap.

Or walkway, as the case may be.

Stomping over to her house, I make a straight line to the front door, where I ring the bell more than necessary.

That'll get her moving.

Sure enough, the door swings open almost immediately.

"What the hell, Hayden?" Addison snaps as she stands there in a fuzzy pale blue sweater, black leggings, and socks. "There's no need to ring the doorbell a hundred times."

I ignore her gripe.

I'm glad it bothered her.

That was my intention.

"Here," I say flatly. "This was lying on my walkway. It's addressed to you."

I hand her the package, which she tosses inside.

Okay, she's mad.

Crossing her arms, she huffs. "You could have just left that on my doorstep, you know?"

I laugh sarcastically. "And where would be the fun in that, *sweetheart*?"

Glaring at me, she grinds out, "Are you here just to irritate me?"

"No. I'm here to ask why you're being so ridiculous."

"Ridiculous?" she barks. "In what way would that be?"

"Seriously?" My brows shoot up. "Where should I start? Oh, I know. How about you taking an innocent situation and just seeing what you want to see? Or what about you not even entertaining that what I told you actually happened is the truth?" I'm on a roll as I add, "You know what I think, Addison?"

Not nearly as snarky as she was a minute ago, she says quietly, "What's that?"

"I think you're afraid."

Her eyes flash in ire. "Oh, this should be good. Do share. What am I afraid of, Hayden?"

I hold her gaze as I tell her, "You're afraid of us, of our potential. I think you got spooked by something so real that you blew the first thing that came up out of proportion. Maybe it is better that we're finished."

A pained expression crosses her face, but I refuse to back down. It doesn't last long, though.

Right in front of my eyes, her hurt turns to rage. "Yeah," she says icily. "Maybe it is good we're finished. We clearly make a rotten couple."

Ouch!

She goes on. "And for the record, you're wrong. I didn't get 'spooked.' I just can't believe you even gave Kristi the time of day. She fucking threw you under the bus, Hayden."

Cold as ice now myself, I retort, "No, sweetheart, as I recall, *you* did that."

Leaving her stunned and speechless, I spin around and walk away.

Chapter

Thirty

ADDISON

As Hayden stomps off, I slam the door shut as hard as I can. "Take that, you fucker!"

I am so mad at that man right now.

He clearly won that round with his turning the tables on me.

Grrr...

Why does he always have to get the last word in?

And to think I was actually kind of excited to see him on my doorstep, despite his ringing the bell like a lunatic and aggravating me.

But then he had to be a jerk and irritate me further.

That man knows exactly which buttons to push.

Of course, once he started up, I had to as well.

It's always that way with us.

I guess we're too much alike. We both always have to be right.

But is he correct about me being afraid?

Ahh, there's the million-dollar question.

Did I make a big deal out of him talking with Kristi because I was looking for a way to push him away?

Shit, maybe.

Sighing, I take the package upstairs, where I open it in my bedroom only to find it's some new leggings I bought.

Setting the garments aside, I grab the packaging to take downstairs to throw away.

On the way down the carpeted steps, I'm beyond distracted. I'm still thinking about Hayden and everything he said.

I'm so in another world that I miss the next-to-last step, and—*wham!*—I twist my left ankle on the bottom stair, promptly landing on my ass.

"Ow, ow, ow."

Seated at the base of the staircase, I lift up and rub my sore butt. It aches, yeah, but I have some padding there. I'll be all right.

What really hurts is my ankle.

I attempt to stand and...nope.

I sit right the hell back down on the thankfully carpeted floor.

What am I going to do now?

My ankle really freaking hurts.

Should I even try to put weight on it?

I don't want to make it worse.

Looking around, I notice my phone is on a stand at the base of the staircase next to me.

Yes, it's within reach!

Well, more or less.

I have to kneel to reach up and grab it, which I do, making my ankle promptly protest.

Damn.

I sit back down on the floor, phone in hand.

Contemplating my options, I tap the device to my chin.

I'm in a dilemma.

I'm not in enough pain to warrant a call to 9-1-1. But I need some sort of assistance.

Unfortunately, there's really only one person I can call for help—the man who I'm sure does not want to hear from me after our argument.

But he's my only hope.

Sighing, I call Hayden.

And he answers right away.

Maybe he's not that angry with me after all?

"Addison?" he says in a questioning tone.

"Yeah, it's me." I blow out a breath.

"Calling me on purpose?" he snarks. "Or did you butt-dial my number?"

Well, maybe he is still a little pissed.

Undeterred, I go on. "Ha ha ha, you're real funny. And yes, I'm calling you intentionally."

"Okay…" Now he sounds hesitant.

I don't want him to hang up on me, so I hurry up and say, "I have a little situation going on over here, and I may need some assistance."

"Really?" he says slowly. "What kind of situation are we talking about?"

I can't tell if he's concerned or aggravated, so I just blurt out, "Okay, I know you hate me right now, but I tripped coming down the stairs, and I think I might've really hurt my ankle. I don't want to get up and hobble around and make it any worse. If you could just stop over, even for a few minutes, and help me into the living room, that'd be great. Oh, and maybe you can grab me some ice from the freezer.

Then I should be good."

I finally take a breath, and he says softly, "First, Addison, I don't hate you. You know that. And second, I'll be over in a minute."

"Thank you," I murmur before we disconnect.

And then, leaning back on the bottom step, I wait for Hayden.

Chapter

Thirty-One

HAYDEN

Addison is hurt and needs me. That's all that matters. All of the anger and irritation I felt toward her dissolved the second she told me she's injured.

I slip on a pair of athletic shoes and race out of my house, cutting across our lawns. In no time, I'm tapping in the code on her security pad.

It beeps, and I open the door and step in.

"Hey," Addison says, waving to me from the floor at the base of the stairs.

"Babe…" I rush over, kneeling in front of her. "Are you okay? Is your ankle the only thing that's bothering you?"

"Yeah." She nods. "Pretty much. I landed on my ass, and that's a little achy, but my ankle is what really hurts like hell."

"Okay." I catch her gaze. "Is it all right if I look at it?"

She nods, and I slip off her fuzzy sock. "Damn. It's definitely swollen."

Slipping my hand down to cup her heel, I gently turn her foot, testing her ankle.

She immediately pulls back. "Ouch!"

"I'm sorry, I'm sorry." Sighing, I say, "Maybe we should take you to the ER or an urgent care and have your ankle x-rayed."

"Do we really have to?" she asks. "I really don't want to make a big deal out of this if it's not too badly injured. Can't we just put some ice on it for now and give it a little time?"

I think it over and come up with a better solution. "How about if I call our trainer, Rob, and ask him if he can come over? He has years of experience with all kinds of injuries. He can tell us right away if you need to go to the ER or if we can just take care of it right here."

Addison nods. "I like that idea. I'm good with it."

"Perfect."

Taking out my phone, I call Rob.

He answers, and after I explain the situation, he agrees to come over.

I give him the address, and we disconnect.

"He's on his way," I tell Addison. Then, standing, I say, "I'm going to get some ice for you from the freezer. I'll wrap it in a kitchen towel, and we can put it on your ankle to take down the swelling."

"Okay," she replies. "I actually have an ice pack in there."

"Perfect." I turn toward the kitchen. "I'll grab that, wrap it, and be right back."

I start to walk away but skid to a halt when Addison calls out quietly, "Hayden?"

I take a step back and look down at her. "Yeah?"

With no hint of sarcasm, and looking up at me with sad green eyes, she murmurs, "Thank you."

In that moment, I know we'll be okay.

Not just Addison and her ankle but us as a couple.

The trainer arrives within the next half hour. He rings the doorbell as I'm sitting next to Addison on the floor at the base of the steps.

Yeah, we're still in the same spot, just chatting like nothing ever happened.

I suggested we move to the living room after I brought in the ice pack, reminding her that the sofa would be much more comfortable. But she insisted she didn't want to get up and move around until she gets the go-ahead from a medical professional.

Well, Rob is that. He really has seen a, like, million injuries like this one. He'll be able to assess Addison's twisted ankle in no time.

After I let him in and introductions are made, he drops to the floor to get to work.

I stand close enough to see what's going on, but I make sure to stay out of the way.

After moving the ice pack aside to assess the swelling, Rob feels around all over Addison's ankle area.

"Does that hurt?" he asks, turning her foot this way and that just like I did.

She doesn't pull away like she did with me, but she does wince a lot. "Yes," she bites out. "It hurts, but not in a way like things feel broken."

"Hmmm, okay." He nods. "That's a good sign. I don't think anything is broken either."

While Rob continues, I blow out a relieved breath.

Once he's done with his examination, he stands and tells us both,

"As I said, nothing appears to be broken. It's just a bad sprain. Still, if the pain gets any worse, or doesn't get any better, I'd recommend having it x-rayed."

"Okay." Addison nods, and then she asks, "Is it all right to move around?"

He chuckles. "Yes, of course. But I want you to follow the RICE protocol—rest, ice, compression, and elevation. What I recommend is for you to take it easy for the next few days. Apply ice four-to-six times a day for twenty-minute intervals until the swelling goes down. Keep your leg elevated when you're seated or lying down. As for the compression, I have an Aircast in my truck. I'll grab that and also bring you in a set of crutches. You might want to use them to get around for a couple of days. That way you won't apply any undue pressure to your ankle while it's healing."

"I can do all that," Addison replies. "Thank you."

"You're welcome," Rob says. "I'm glad I could help. Now let me run out to my truck and get those items."

While Rob leaves to grab the Aircast and crutches, Addison finally lets me help her into the living room.

It feels good to have my arm wrapped around her and to have her leaning into me. I've missed being close with her.

After Addison is settled in the crook of one side of the sofa, I meet Rob back at the front door. He hands me the cast and crutches, and after I thank him, he leaves.

I take everything into the living room, setting the crutches close by.

Holding up the Aircast, I ask, "Do you want me to put this on for you?"

"Yeah," Addison says, holding up her ice pack. "I think it's time for a break from icing, anyway."

"Probably," I agree.

I take a seat down by her feet and strap on the Aircast, which is essentially two cushioned plastic braces supported by a piece of cloth that goes under the heel of her foot and then is secured with Velcro around the calf.

Once I'm done fastening her cast, I slip a throw pillow under her foot and stand up. "There. I think you're all set."

"What now?" she asks, peering up at me sorrowfully.

I don't want to make any assumptions, so I hedge, "Um, I guess I'll go back over to my house."

Blinking like she might start to cry, she asks, "Can you stay with me for a little while, Hayden?"

I'm actually relieved she's asking, as I don't want to leave her alone, certainly not when she's clearly down and out physically and emotionally.

"Of course I'll stay," I say with a smile.

Even if she wasn't injured, there's nowhere else I'd rather be than right here with the woman I love.

Chapter

Thirty-Two

ADDISON

I don't know why, but I feel so emotional. I'm truly about to cry. And I sure as hell don't want to be alone. I also don't want just anyone here with me—I want Hayden.

He's the one, and it's always going to be him.

Yeah, I'm in deep—I love him so much. And tonight I'm finally going to tell him. No more just mouthing the words when he can't see my face. No more waiting for the right moment.

There's never going to be a time like the present.

So after Hayden says, "Of course I'll stay," I ask him to sit down next to me on the sofa.

He hesitates as I lower my legs and place my feet on the floor—carefully, of course.

"You should keep that foot elevated," he says, staring down at my ankle.

"I know, and I will." I pat the space next to me. "But just sit here with me for a minute. I want to tell you something. It's important."

"Okay." As he takes a seat, he looks concerned and adds softly, "Babe, you're worrying me. Is there something else going on?"

"Nothing bad," I assure him with a laugh.

He's so sweet, worrying about me like this. And the way he came to my aid earlier, with no questions or hesitation. Our earlier argument now just seems silly. I'm glad he didn't hold it against me.

Thinking about his amazing response to my mishap, calling the team trainer and everything, I take his hand in mine. "Hayden..."

As I take a deep breath, his pale blue eyes meet my gaze. "Yes?"

Exhaling quickly, I say in a rush, "I know this isn't the most romantic of circumstances, but there's probably never going to be a perfect time. Even if there were, I'm tired of waiting. The simple fact is, Hayden Harrington, you drive me crazy sometimes, and you certainly know how to push all of my buttons, both good"—I waggle my brows—"and bad, but I freaking love your annoying, and also hot and sexy, ass."

First he looks shocked, but then it dawns on him what I just said.

Suppressing a big-ass smile, he volleys back, "Wow. You love my ass, huh?"

I smack his arm. "Stop it. You know what I mean."

"I know, sweetheart." Scooting closer, he takes my face in his hands. "Addison Knight, you are the woman for me. I've known it for a while now. You make me want to be a better man, though I know I'm definitely a work in progress. That being said, I want to be my best for you, because, babe, I fucking love you too."

His lips crash down on mine, and it's our best kiss yet—hot, passionate, and filled with the love we just declared for each other.

We don't stop or slow down.

It's like we can't get enough.

He lifts me and carries me upstairs to the bedroom, where clothes are discarded and bodies are joined.

Hayden is careful with my ankle, but it doesn't matter. Nothing hurts in this moment.

No, every part of my body feels amazing, especially when he works me with his hands, his tongue, and his glorious cock.

"Ahhhh…" I fall apart beneath him, taking him with me.

Afterward, we lie wrapped up together until we must have each other once again.

This is our love being expressed, and it feels like we might never leave this bed.

Chapter

Thirty-Three

HAYDEN

Addison tells me she doesn't ever want to leave the bed, and I feel the same way. I could love her like this forever.

But there comes a time that we have to stop.

We wear each other out, at least for the time being. Plus, I'm concerned about her ankle. We've been careful, but she really should get some rest and ice and elevate it again.

The other issue that arises is that we're both starving, as neither of us ever had any dinner.

So, after cleaning up and slipping our clothes back on, we make our way down to the living room.

Actually, I carry Addison.

Yeah, I'm not about to let her hobble down the stairs and take another chance on falling.

"Are you going to carry me up and down the stairs all the time now?" she asks with a chuckle as I set her down on the sofa.

"As long as I'm around, yes." I slip the throw pillow under her ankle as she gets settled. "At least I plan to until your foot starts feeling better."

"Okay." She smiles. "I'm not going to fight you on that one."

"Finally, something we agree on," I tease.

She laughs. "I know, right?"

I sit on the coffee table and take her hand in mine. "Hey, speaking of fights and disagreements, I'm sorry I didn't say anything to you sooner about talking with Kristi."

Waving her free hand, she says, "Hayden, forget about it. It's all water under the bridge. But for what it's worth, I'm sorry for not giving you the benefit of the doubt. I overreacted. And I think you were right—I was just scared."

Softly, I ask, "You're not scared now, are you?"

"No." She shakes her head. "I'm not."

Smiling at her, I say, "I guess our whole fight could have been avoided if we'd just let each other talk."

"Probably, but we're learning."

"We are," I agree. And then I add, "Hey, there's something I wanted to tell you."

"What's that?"

I'm practically bursting with joy when I share, "I got the land."

"Holy crap!" She squeezes my hand. "That is so awesome, Hayden."

"I think so, too, babe."

"So when can you start having a house built?"

I blow out a breath. "After all the papers are signed and it's official. I'm thinking by the beginning of the new year."

"This is so great," she murmurs.

Addison is beaming, and it touches my heart that she's so happy for me. But I don't want to do this alone. It really means nothing without her.

I tell her as much, and then I add, "I want your input every step of the way."

She nods excitedly. "I can do that. I think it'll be fun sharing ideas."

"That's exactly what I'm thinking too."

I actually want more. I see a clear future with Addison, and I want her to eventually move in with me. That's another reason why I want her opinions and input. She needs to love the house. I know she likes the property, but she should feel at home there as much as I hope to.

I don't want to put it all out there today, though.

I'm going to wait for the right time.

Besides, I just heard her stomach growl, and I'm fucking famished as well.

So, letting go of her hand, I ask, "Now, what should we do for food?"

She thinks it over for a beat and throws out, "How about we order pizza?"

"Sounds perfect." I stand, taking my phone from the back pocket of my jeans.

Together, we take a look at the online menu and decide to order a pepperoni pizza and breadsticks with sauce.

While we wait for the food to arrive, and after I retrieve her more ice from the kitchen—this time just cubes wrapped in a tea towel since we forgot to put her ice pack back in the freezer earlier—Addison tells me about the great response she's heard all week regarding my feature in *Atlanta Sports Monthly*.

She says, "I set up a few more interviews for you and a couple of online hockey outlet features. They're all reputable and have lots of subscribers, so you should get some good exposure."

"Fantastic," I reply, feeling genuinely grateful. "Thanks. Things are really working out, huh?"

"They are," she agrees. "They really, really are."

We both mean more than just the two of us successfully rebuilding my image. We mean us—as a couple, as partners, as everything good two people can be.

The pizza arrives, and we eat it while watching a movie.

Afterward, we head upstairs to bed, where we curl up together.

Addison falls asleep where I want her to be every possible night—in my arms.

Chapter

Thirty-Four

ADDISON

Hayden spends the rest of the weekend at my house. He only leaves me for practice Saturday morning and to run over to his house to pick up more clothes.

Oh, and he sticks to his promise of carrying me up and down the stairs, even when I tell him by Sunday night that my ankle is already feeling better.

"Seriously," I say as I shift on the sofa, "I was originally thinking I'd take a day or two off from work, but I feel good enough that I'm just going to go in."

"What about driving?" Hayden asks.

He's seated down from me, with my feet elevated on a pillow in his lap. I'm done with icing, and I'm only wearing the Aircast when I'm up and about.

"I only need my right foot to drive," I remind him. "It's my left ankle that's hurt."

He nods. "Good point."

"Yeah, I have it all planned out. I have some nice flats I can wear, and with the holidays coming up, everyone is dressing more casually anyway."

"Oh, speaking of the holidays…" Hayden says.

"Yes?"

"The team Christmas party is this Saturday night. I was thinking, if you feel up for it, it'd be a perfect opportunity to let everyone know we're a couple."

I'm excited, as I'm ready to let our relationship status be known to the world. Well, at least our world.

"Yes," I say, smiling happily, "I love that idea."

"Great." He pats my thigh. "I do too. Then—" He laughs. "—I can finally take you out on a real date."

Pointing at him, but just in good fun, I tell him, "I'm going to hold you to that, buddy."

Hayden is completely serious, though, when he replies, "Addison, this is just the beginning. I'm making you a promise right here and now that I am going to treat you like a queen."

"Wow." Kicking away the pillow with my good foot, I curl my finger and beckon him to me. "Come here."

Once he settles his weight on me, I look up at him and ask, "Do you know how much I love you?"

Brushing his lips over mine, he murmurs, "I have an idea, but I think you better show me."

"Yeah, I think so too."

I then do exactly that.

Throughout the week, the Thunder have only two games—one on Monday and another on Thursday. Since both are home matchups, Hayden and I are able to spend all of our free time together.

Yay!

There's more good news too. My ankle feels significantly better by Friday. Maybe it wasn't such a bad sprain after all. Still, even though I ditched the crutches and the Aircast, I wear flats all week to work.

And I take it easy.

On the way home from the office on Friday, I stop at a specialty dress shop to pick up a stunning kelly green sequined formfitting gown I ordered online for the team Christmas party that's tomorrow night.

The associate who helps me suggests a cute pair of black velvet flats to pair with the dress.

Perfect.

Her suggestion turns out to be spot-on. Once I'm dressed on Saturday night, only the toes of the flats peek out from under the dress. No one will even realize I'm not wearing heels.

Hayden picks me up at seven, and damn, does he ever look amazingly hot in his black tux with velvet trim. I can barely keep my eyes off of him as he drives us to the team owner's mansion in the Buckhead part of town.

"Wow," I marvel when we pull into a large semicircle driveway.

Yeah, I'm impressed by the giant home in front of me. It's stone and decorated in thousands of clear lights and holiday greenery, accentuated with red bows and ribbons.

This is clearly going to be quite an elegant affair.

A valet comes up to the Cayenne and opens the door for me.

After I step out carefully, Hayden comes around the front of the vehicle and joins me on the side.

"Are you ready?" he asks as we begin to make our way up a wide set of stone steps leading to opulently carved wooden double doors.

I know he's referring to our debut as a couple.

Glancing over at him, I reply, "I am. I'm excited."

"Good." He takes my hand. "I am too."

He knocks, and a butler opens the door. The sound of chatter and low music can be heard immediately, indicating the party is well underway.

As we step inside, the butler welcomes us and hands us each a flute of champagne. He then directs us to the ballroom.

"Down the hall and to the right," he says in a crisp British accent. "That's where you'll find the party."

"Thank you," Hayden replies.

We head down the hall, the muffled sound of chatter, laughter, and light music growing louder.

Before we step into the ballroom, I take Hayden's arm. "Still want to do this?" I ask.

"Hell, yeah." He laughs. "I want the world to know we're in love."

"Good. I do too."

Together, we walk in.

The party is crowded, which gives us time to get our bearings.

But then Coach Barnes notices us. His brows go up, and he starts smiling as he makes his way over.

Chuckling, he nods to me and pats Hayden on the back. "Hmm, looks like you two have been keeping a secret."

Hayden glances around, as do I. It's clear from the growing number of stares and raised eyebrows that his teammates are beginning to realize we're a couple.

Jerking his chin to the crowd, Hayden says, "Looks like it's not going to be a secret for too much longer."

"No." Coach laughs. "I think not."

Hey, it's all good.

This is what we want.

And it turns out to be amazing. As we mingle, we discover everyone is really happy for us. A lot of folks are surprised, as well.

The only two who are in the know, of course, are Arden and Nils. Since they're really Hayden's two best friends on the team, we hang out with them the most, especially as the night wears on. We even find ourselves a cool little nook off the ballroom with high-backed chairs and a massive ten-foot decorated tree.

That becomes our spot for the duration.

At one point, though, we run out of champagne. Since there are no waiters daring to intrude on our private space, even though we wouldn't mind, Nils and Hayden decide to go grab us more champagne.

Arden and I are left alone, and the subject of the land Hayden is buying comes up.

"How do you like living out there?" I ask him.

"Ahh, Addison, I love it." He leans back in his chair. "I told Hayden a while back that even though it's a hike to the arena, it's worth it to be so close to nature and have all that peace and solitude."

"It is a beautiful area," I agree. And then I add, "Though now you'll have a new neighbor. I mean, once the house is built."

With a sly smile, he retorts, "Hmm, I'm thinking maybe I'll have *two* new neighbors."

Surprised, I point to myself. "Do you mean me?"

He laughs. "Of course I mean you. And I bet it's not that far off."

I shrug. "Who knows? You could be right."

It's true. If my relationship with Hayden continues to progress—and I feel certain it will—moving in together would be the next logical step.

And then what?

Marriage, maybe kids?

Yikes, am I ready for all that?

You know what?

I am.

I'm no longer hesitant or afraid.

I love Hayden, and I want a long life with him.

And that includes everything that goes with it.

Chapter

Thirty-Five

HAYDEN

Over the Christmas holiday, Addison and I meet each other's families.

We fly to Pittsburgh first, after a home game on the twenty-third, and drive up to the little town of Butler, where she's from, to spend Christmas Eve with her parents and her sister, Willow.

As soon as I meet her family, I am stunned by how much Addison takes after her father. She has his same raven-black hair and emerald eyes.

Conversely, Willow is a carbon copy of her mother—strawberry-blonde hair and piercing blue eyes.

Everyone is personable, and I feel at home right away.

At dinner, the subject of Willow having one more semester of college comes up. She tells me she'll graduate with a degree in business finance in May.

"Have you thought about applying with the Thunder?" Addison

asks her. "I'd love to have you living in the same city as me."

Willow nods excitedly. "That would be fun. If I do apply, can you put in a good word for me?"

"Of course," Addison says, laughing.

I chime in and tell her I'll do the same.

She responds, "Wow, thank you, Hayden. That means a lot."

These people already feel like family, and in that moment, I know in my heart they someday will be.

Addison, seated next to me, squeezes my thigh under the table. "That was really sweet of you," she murmurs softly so only I can hear. "I'll have to thank you properly later."

She winks, and, clearing my throat, I take a quick sip of water.

Damn, this woman.

She's so naughty and fun.

I love her more with each passing day.

On Christmas morning, we say goodbye to her family and take a short flight up to Buffalo, where we spend the day with my parents, my brother, and his wife.

Addison gets along and fits in perfectly with our crazy clan. There's a lot of joking around and good-natured teasing.

She tells me that night, "Now I see where you get that smart mouth from."

"Hey," I volley back, chuckling. "You kept up with us."

Looking pleased with herself, she murmurs, "I kind of did, huh?"

"Babe, you definitely did."

Our time with our families gets me to thinking, on the way home the next day, how I really want a life with Addison, and I want it to start soon.

So, after we land in Atlanta and are driving away from the airport, I ask her, "Do you mind if we stop up at the property I bought?"

All the legal paperwork has gone through, so it's officially mine now.

"Sure." She nods as she shrugs off her heavy winter coat. It's a fairly mild day down here in the south. I took off my jacket as soon as we got into the car. "It's beautiful up there," Addison goes on. "I always love stopping by."

That puts a smile on my face. I love how she and I are always on the same page these days.

The drive goes quickly since there's very little traffic, and in no time, we're pulling up and parking in front of my property.

"Are you up for a walk?" I ask her.

"Always," she replies.

We're dressed in jeans and hiking boots, and though we ditched the winter coats, we still have on sweaters over long-sleeved turtlenecks.

I meet Addison on her side of my Porsche, and we walk the perimeter of the open space where my house will be built.

Clearing my throat, I glance over at her. "Hey, I wanted to tell you I have an architect sending over a bunch of ideas for the house."

"What kind of ideas?" she asks.

"All the design stuff—styling, layout, materials, just about everything you can think of."

She blows out a breath. "You sure are going to have a lot of decisions to make."

"Yeah, you're right about that." I slow to a stop and turn her to face me. "But I don't want to make them alone, Addison. I want your input on everything."

"I'll help you, sure." She nods. "But ultimately it's your house, Hayden."

My eyes meet hers as I ask, "What if I don't want it to be?"

Biting her lip, she asks carefully, "What do you mean?"

"I mean"—I take her hands in mine—"I want it to be your house too. I guess what I'm saying is will you move in with me?"

Laughing, she says, "Yes, I'd love to live with you. And you know what? Arden called this."

I cock my head. "How do you mean?"

"Well, I mentioned to him at the Christmas party how he'll soon be having a new neighbor, meaning you. He said he had a feeling he'd be having two new neighbors."

Nodding approvingly, I state, "He's a wise man, that Arden."

She giggles. "He is."

We continue our walk around the property, and every step of the way, we talk about what *we* want in *our* new house.

But really, it's not just going to be a house.

It'll be a home—our home.

And hopefully it will be for a long, long time.

Chapter

Thirty-Six

ADDISON

I know after Christmas that Hayden is my future.

I never thought someone you once despised so much could end up becoming the love of your life.

But it can happen.

I'm living proof, as it happened to me.

Sometimes I think all that anger was just us masking deeper feelings we didn't want to face.

I mean, there was always an intense attraction, even when we didn't get along.

Maybe we always sensed something more—like…potential.

After all, we are a lot alike.

We always have to be right.

And we also have to get in the last word.

That's why we sometimes fight.

But now our fights are resolved in the bedroom.

Damn, making up is so much fun.

Still, I guess the biggest trait we share is that we love to win.

And on that subject, though Hayden will dispute me that he's the biggest winner in our relationship, I'll always believe that I came out ahead.

I won in the game of love when I met that man.

It just took us a while to get here.

Epilogue

HAYDEN

While we wait for our dream home to be built, Addison moves into my rental house before her lease is up.

We get a preview of what it's like living together, and it goes really fucking well.

Sure, we still banter and spar—we always will—but we never go to bed angry.

One thing we bicker about is who came out the bigger winner in the relationship. She thinks she did, but we all know it's me. Addison makes me a better person. She *is* my life.

That's why, in the spring, before it's time to move into our "real" home, I know without a doubt that I want more from her.

I want Addison Knight to be my wife.

I think of all the ways I could propose—public or private, flashy or low-key.

There are so many options.

But in the end, I decide I'll do like we always do—I'll ask her when the time feels right.

That time comes one night when we're wrapped up in a checkered flannel blanket, chilling on a big sheepskin rug, in front of a roaring fire in the living room.

We're drinking champagne, for no other reason than to just celebrate life.

I recently got back from a long string of road games. Addison was so happy to see me when I stepped into the house. She was literally vibrating with energy and excitement when I wrapped her up in my arms for the best fucking hug.

Yeah, I fucking missed her too.

That was earlier, and since then, I knew this would be the night I propose.

I even prepared by slipping the engagement ring I bought a few weeks ago into my jeans pocket.

Now I'm just waiting for the perfect moment...

My opportunity comes when Addison slides out of our blanket cocoon to take a quick bathroom break.

Standing and pointing at me before she walks away, she says, "I'll be right back. Don't go anywhere."

"Oh, don't worry." I laugh. "I am here to stay."

I mean that in so many fucking ways.

Once Addison is out of sight, I sit up and dig the platinum ring with the big, sparkly diamond solitaire from my pocket.

It sure is a beauty, I think as I plop it into Addison's half-full champagne flute.

The damn diamond is so big, there's no way she won't notice it.

I am a little worried, though, that she'll see it before she's snuggled back in the blanket with me.

But my concern is unfounded.

When she returns, she doesn't even look at the flute.

No, she's looking at me.

"What?" I ask, cocking a brow as I peer up at her.

Standing above me with a smile on her face, she says, "I was just thinking about how much I love you."

"I love you, too, babe." I pat the sheepskin rug. "Now come back down here and join me."

After she does, I wrap her back up in the blanket with me.

Finally, she reaches for her champagne. "Whoa, wait, what? Hayden..."

"Yes?"

I'm suppressing the biggest grin, as this is going just as I planned.

Slowly, she picks up the flute and stares inside, musing, "There's a ring in my champagne."

I chuckle. "Yes, there is."

"What does it mean?"

She's so cute.

I say, "Well, first, I think you should take it out. And then we'll get to what it means."

Once she fishes the ring out, I gently slip it from her hand.

Rising to my knees, the blanket falling down around us, I turn to her.

Holding out the ring, and with all my heart and soul, I say, "Addison, I love you beyond all my wildest dreams. But to make my very best dream come true, I'm asking you to marry me."

Looking stunned, she murmurs, "You are?"

I laugh. "Yes, sweetheart, I am."

It's like it hits her then, and she says happily, "Hayden, marrying you is my best dream too. So, yes, I will absolutely, positively become your wife."

"Babe…" My heart soars as I slip the ring on her finger.

We then seal our love with a perfect, passionate kiss.

We have so much to look forward to—moving into our new home, announcing our engagement, planning a wedding.

And then what?

Children?

Yeah, I can see that.

But for now, I'm reveling in the fact that my best dream has just come true.

I'm marrying Addison—my best friend, my lover, my life.

We have so much ahead of us.

We have today, tomorrow, and the rest of our lives.

The End

Up next in this new *Breakaway Hockey* romance series of interconnected standalones is book #2—*Arden*—releasing October 2023!

About The Author

S.R. Grey is a USA Today Bestselling Author of the new Breakaway hockey series and the popular Boys of Winter hockey books and Men of Fall football novels. Other New Adult and Romantic Suspense works of hers include the Judge Me Not books, the Promises series, the Inevitability duology, A Harbour Falls Mystery trilogy, and the Laid Bare series of novellas.Ms. Grey resides in Pennsylvania. When not writing, she can be found reading, traveling, running, or cheering for her hometown sports teams, sometimes all at the same time.

Visit S.R. Grey's Author Website (if for nothing else, because it's pretty!): srgrey.com/

S.R. Grey on Facebook is a hoot: www.facebook.com/SRGrey

S.R. Grey's FB Reading Group is even more fun: www.facebook.com/groups/SRGreyHardAbsandHotBooks/

Sign-up to receive her exciting Author Newsletter (you know you want to): mad.ly/signups/106801/join

Follow S.R. Grey on BookBub for selected Sales Updates: www.bookbub.com/authors/s-r-grey

Follow S.R. Grey on Twitter for randomness: twitter.com/AuthorSRGrey

Follow S.R. Grey on Instagram for the riveting pics (well, at least she thinks so): www.instagram.com/authorsrgrey/

S.R. Grey Goodreads Author page: www.goodreads.com/author/show/6433082.S_R_Grey

Wait!

It's not over yet.

Check out the first chapter of **Destiny on Ice,** the beginning of the bestselling *Boys of Winter* hockey rom-com series.

ONE

GOLDEN BOY GETS A LITTLE TARNISHED

BRENT

My father was a great hockey player. Back in the day, in the era of eighties' big hair and synthesized music, Billy Oliver won not just one, but two Stanley Cups. He was awarded the Conn Smythe trophy both times and has received an assortment of other hardware throughout the years.

He's retired now, but my dad was once a star.

To me, though, he's always just been Dad.

But as his only child, I have a legacy to live up to. I pray I don't disappoint him. I pray someday I'll be as good as he once was. And damn it, I better win a freaking Stanley Cup like he did.

I have no choice, not really. Since the moment my father first laced up hockey skates on my three-year-old little feet, the look of pride on his face told me even then all I needed to know—anything short of being the best will never do.

And guess what?

In many ways, I've become the best at what I do, which is, like my dad, play professional hockey.

I've been good since the start, a natural some say. I don't know about that, but I do know that even before I was drafted—in the first round by the Las Vegas Wolves, an expansion team at the time—I was being called "The Golden Boy" and "The Next One."

These days, three years later, I'm pretty much the poster boy for the NHL. And I have a slew of endorsement deals to prove it.

Lately, though, I've been falling short.

And I really don't know why.

Something is missing for me in the game. Or is it something that's missing in *me*?

I blow out a breath and shake my head.

Things started out so great. Where'd it all go wrong?

I made a name for myself early on. Expansion teams usually struggle for years before posting a winning record. Not so for the Wolves. With me centering what was then a subpar line, I was still able to make us shine. We came out swinging that first season in the league.

BRENT OLIVER SCORES THE GAME-WINNING GOAL IN HIS AND THE WOLVES' FIRST NHL GAME, SETS UP TEAMMATES FOR TWO MORE

One month later, there was this:

THE WOLVES OFF TO A COMPLETELY UNEXPECTED STELLAR START

Then things started to slide.

Those subpar players on my line weren't enough to keep afloat a pretty much overall crappy team, even with me centering. The Wolves' owners and management made the necessary moves—they don't mess around when shit needs to get done.

We picked up a phenomenal winger, Nolan Solvenson. He started to play and things turned around.

ADDING SKILLED RIGHT-WINGER NOLAN SOLVENSON TO ROOKIE BRENT OLIVER'S FIRST LINE PROVING TO BE A MASTERFUL MOVE
ON A MID-SEASON WINNING STREAK, THAT SOLVENSON TRADE IS PAYING OFF FOR THE WOLVES!

Another trade made at the deadline gave us Benjamin Perry. A big, strong left-handed winger, he was the final piece to the puzzle. Even with far-from-elite second, third, and fourth lines, it didn't matter. Not with me, Benjamin, and Nolan on the first line. We could *not* be stopped.

Benjamin—or Benny, as he's known to the team—is adept at using his size and muscle to check the hell out of any sorry soul who happens to be matched up against him. He simply wears other players down…and then it's a fucking scorefest. Thanks, in part, to his killer slapshot.

Together with Nolan, a sniper in his own right, we were—and in many ways still are—quite a force to be reckoned with. We destroy teams, though not as much lately. But back then, man, we were racking up so many points that the press branded us the OPS line, as in Special Forces.

THE OPS LINE'S SNIPERS OF OLIVER, PERRY, AND SOLVENSON ELIMINATE THE COMPETITION WITH EASE
THERE'S NOTHING COVERT ABOUT THIS LINE'S SCORING PROWESS

We worked our reputation to our advantage. Trash-talking on the ice and taunting players became our pastimes. We also happened to get a lot of pucks in the net.

Ah, the good old days.

We still trash-talk and taunt, but we aren't as lethal as we once were.

"We just need to get back on track," I murmur to myself. "The season doesn't start for a few more weeks. I'll have my shit together by then."

I better, since I'm the captain of the team. If I go down, we all sink. And that's not fair to anyone, especially not to my linemates, Nolan and Benny. Over the past couple of years they've become my best friends, which is a blessing and a curse. It's a blessing that we play so well together, but it's a curse that we also have a tendency to fuel each other's vices.

God knows this off-season we've become far too focused on partying and women. Like me, my linemates are extremely popular. Hell, let's not mince words—we're gods. In the hockey world, it's good to be a god. Guys want to *be* you and girls want to *do* you. Multiply that all by a hundred if you're not an ogre in the looks department.

And none of us are.

Not to brag—though, I guess I kind of am—but I have the most women falling at my feet. Hell, I've had women who've wanted to *lick* my feet.

Like, literally.

There was this crazy bitch this one time…

Wait, I digress. Back to where our team is today—floundering in a sea of mediocrity.

After that first good regular season, we fell apart during the playoffs. A dirty hit that sent me flying into the boards also sidelined me with a concussion. It didn't end there. More bad luck plagued our team. Nolan went into a scoring slump, and Benny took a punishing check against the boards that broke his foot. We were knocked out of the playoffs in the first round.

I went to Minneapolis, my hometown, to sulk.

"Next year will be different," my always-positive father tried to reassure me.

He was wrong.

We missed the playoffs entirely the following year, for reasons still unknown.

Then there was the season that just ended this past spring—another disappointment.

LAS VEGAS WOLVES FOLD, KNOCKED OUT ONCE AGAIN IN THE FIRST ROUND

Needing a break from all things desert-life, I said to Nolan and Benny, "Fuck this shit."

That was over three months ago. We were in the middle of cleaning out our lockers for the summer. My linemates looked at me, confused.

And then Nolan finally asked, "Fuck what shit, Oliver? What are you going on about over there?"

"Everything," I replied, gesturing around the empty locker room. "We're done, finished. Let's get the hell out of this place for a while."

I meant Las Vegas the city—and I think Nolan was catching my drift—but Benny misunderstood.

"Dude," Benny began, "we *better* get outta here soon." He checked his watch. "We have a tee time at two."

He meant the golf game we had planned, but I was having none of that.

"Fuck golfing," I snapped. "I'm talking about *really* getting out of here. I think we deserve a much-needed break from this whole damn town."

Nolan looked intrigued. "What'd you have in mind?"

I happily shared with him and Benny what I'd been thinking about for days. "Let's head up to my house in Minnesota. We can spend the summer on the lake." I grinned, bad intentions in mind. "You know I'm a fucking rock star up there. We can party every night. Hell, we can fuck and get fucked up till training camp starts up in September."

Benny was in immediately, but Nolan had to think it over in his thoughtful kind of way.

At last, he said, "Okay, let's do it."

Since that day we've been partying like rock stars. Or, more accurately, like out-of-control hockey players.

We're still on a roll, even though it's August and we have to fly back to Vegas real soon. Until then, however, I've vowed my cool contemporary house by the lake will remain *the* place to party. It's our OPS base for debauchery, after all.

In reality, though, this craziness can't go on. We all know that.

Even wild and crazy Benny had the sense to ask me just last week, "Dude, what should we do?"

"About what?"

I was in the midst of texting a local puck bunny to see if she wanted to meet me for a quickie, so I was a bit distracted.

Benny sighed. "We gotta report to camp in a less than a month. Guess it's time to start thinking about slowing down with the girls, the booze, the—"

I put down my phone and cut him off with a raucous, "Hell no, my friend. We just need to scale it back a little."

"Scale it back in what way?" Nolan, who walked in the room just at that moment, wanted to know.

I shrugged. "Maybe have smaller parties? Maybe drink a little less?"

We all agreed to those things, but we haven't followed through. In the past seven days we've abstained from partying for all of two.

This is so not going to play well with the team. My diet is crap, and I'm nowhere near peak playing shape. Sure, my body looks all lean and cut, meaning you'd never know I wasn't ready to hit the ice rearing to go, but looks can be deceiving. I went out for a run just the other day and came back fucking winded as hell.

That was a first.

Still, I'm confident I can get back into playing shape in no time. It's the inside of my head that's kind of a mess. I just don't fucking care about winning, not anymore. I mean, I do, but I don't. Does that make sense?

Nah, it doesn't to me, either. But I better figure it out, and fast.

Where's my drive to get my shit together? Where's my commitment to winning, my obligation to my players?

I ask myself these things every day now, but I guess the answers are clouded by my drinking copious amounts of alcohol and fucking way too many puck bunnies.

Dad would be so proud—not.

Well, he would be glad I diligently use protection. I haven't gone *that* far off the rails. Still, wrapping my dick up isn't enough to keep management off my ass. My agent already informed me— this morning, in fact—that the Wolves' ownership group has a pretty good idea of what I've been up to, along with my teammates, here in Minneapolis.

I listened half-heartedly when my agent woke me up to say, "Don't blow this off, Brent. Management is *not* happy with you. There's a certain image they expect you to uphold, and you're not doing that."

God forbid I'm not the team's "Golden Boy." I'm "The Next One," remember?

Bullshit, it's all crap.

Coach Townsend called me shortly after I got off the phone with my agent. He had the same warning.

"You don't want the team to take action. You're not going to like what they have in store for you, Brent, if you keep up with this bad behavior."

"Oh, come on," I replied, laughing. "The Wolves can't fire me. And what could be worse than that?"

Coach T chuckled like he knew something.

Hmm...

"I can't worry about that shit today," I said to him. "I'll start cleaning up my act tomorrow."

"Brent..." Coach T sounded doubtful.

"Really, I will," I insisted.

That was a few hours ago. And I plan to make some changes. But maybe not quite yet.

"Before tomorrow gets here," I justify to myself, "we still have the rest of today. And that means there's time for one more party."

I stride into the second-floor living room of my house, a spacious and angled space overlooking the huge lake on my property. Peering out at the crystal blue water, I announce to Benny and Nolan, "Listen up, boys. We're having one final blowout tonight, a party to end all parties."

There's a murmur from Nolan, but nothing from Benny.

"We're going to do this one right," I go on. "We party tonight. But then, when tomorrow arrives, we're done with messing around. We start training full-on."

Yeah, right, a little voice in my head coughs out.

I look around since no one besides my guilty conscience seems to be chiming in.

It's early afternoon and the sun is bathing the room—my favorite, by the way, with the way it juts out over the lake showcasing the floor-to-ceiling windows on two sides and a massive deck with a mile-long view on the other—in a warm summer glow.

Nolan, who is lounging on an easy chair with a beer in his hand, raises his bottle. "I'm in," he says.

His words aren't the least bit slurred, even though he's been drinking straight through since last night's bash.

"And then, yeah," he continues, agreeing with me, "we'll start getting ready for camp."

Despite his ability to suck down alcohol like a fish, Nolan hasn't veered too far off course. Getting back on track won't be hard for him. He's like Mr. Discipline. And he's not fooling anyone, anyway. I caught him working out in my basement gym a few days ago. With the way he was pumping iron I suspect he's been training consistently for a few weeks now.

There's still not been a response from Benny, which is unusual. Dude's always up for a party. He's probably the worst of us when it comes to out-of-control antics.

And that's saying a lot.

"Hey, where's Benny?" I ask Nolan as I scan the shadows of the room.

He nods to a sofa that's been pushed way-ass off to a far corner.

"Oh, I should've known." I chuckle as I take in an eyeful.

Benny is sprawled out on a sofa in the shadows, sleeping like a baby. His massive chest is rising and falling in perfect rhythm with the ticking clock on the stone mantel above his head. Some puck bunny he was fucking around with last night is with him, passed out on top of him.

The sheet covering their naked bodies is hiked up just enough to afford a view of the girl's creamy thigh, which is casually slung over my linemate's muscular, hairy-as-hell leg, and positioned under his semi-exposed junk.

Chuckling at Benny's total lack of modesty, I pick up a throw pillow and lob it at his head—the one that clearly controls all his thinking.

And he scores!

As the pillow makes contact—and how could it not with a pole like that marking my target?—the sheet falls off completely. I get a quick flash of perky tits and tiny ass. And then, shit—a big honking piece of man-meat assaults my eyes.

"Dude," I snort, mock-offended. "You need to cover that shit before you blind us all."

Benny stirs to life. Sitting up, he barks, "What the fuck, Oliver? I was having the best dream ever. That is till you started tossing shit at my balls. "

Nolan lets out a low chuckle. "Only you, Benny, could find a way of using 'tossing' and 'balls' in the same sentence. But really"—he tilts his bottle to Benny's dick—"you need to do what Brent said and cover that shit up."

Throughout this entire brain-draining exchange, the girl wakes up. And damn, she looks young. Letting out a little squeak, not unlike a hamster, she gathers the sheet around her naked self and scurries off to where she seems to think the bathroom is.

I only know this 'cause she's muttering something about having to pee. But the poor girl has no idea where to go. Hamster-girl flies past me, heading down the wrong hallway, the one that leads to my bedroom.

As I rush to retrieve her, I can't help but grumble, "Why in the hell do they always think the damn bathroom's down *my* hall?"

I catch up to and redirect the girl, pointing her in the correct direction. "It's that way, sweetheart," I say in my kindest tone.

No need to be an asshole; the poor thing already looks shell-shocked. Though whether that's due to waking up in a strange house or waking up next to that monstrous thing Benny calls a cock, I have no clue.

"Thanks, Mr. Oliver," she replies.

And then she runs off.

"*Mr.* Oliver?" I shake my head. "What the fuck is up with that? If she thinks I'm old and I'm only twenty-two, then..."

Whoa, wait.

Hurrying back out to the living room and pointing an accusatory finger at Benny, I say, "That chick better be over eighteen, dude. We're in enough trouble already with the team."

Benjamin Perry is twenty-eight, but he likes younger girls. Nothing illegal, so don't get your panties in a bunch. He just happens to favor babes who either look young, or are *just* old enough.

"She's twenty-three," he replies, sounding hurt by my accusation.

"What? Five years past eighteen?" Nolan peers over at me and smirks. "Hey, Oliver, you think Benny is working up to go cougar on us?"

Laughing, I reply, "Seeing as he's on his way to fucking the full spectrum of girls in their twenties, I do indeed think he's secretly working his way up to thirty."

"Small steps," Nolan says.

"Fuck you," Benny interjects. "You're both dickheads."

I put up my hands. "Hey, don't be pissed at me. Take it up with Nolan. He started with the jokes. I only brought up the chick's age for your own protection. I'm always looking out for you, buddy."

"Yeah, you usually are," he concedes. "And thanks for that." He shoots me an apologetic grin. "You really are a good kid at heart."

I shrug, feeling a little self-conscious at being called a kid. But then I see what Benny is up to, preparing to bust my balls.

Sure enough, the next words out of his mouth are "You do know I mean *kid* in a good kind of way. Like maybe"—he smirks—"a *golden boy* sort of style."

"Ha. Ha," I retort. And since he's enjoying yanking my chain far too much, I shoot him the bird. "Shut the fuck up, man."

Benny may give me a hard time, but his underlying sentiment is genuine. What he said about me being a good guy, like a decent person, is true. Despite all the craziness of late, I want nothing but the best for my friends. And just because I've been fucking up my own life lately doesn't mean Benny's and Nolan's lives have to go down the shitter too.

Really, I probably should've never invited them to Minnesota. I should have come up to the lake house by myself. That would've been the smart thing to do, especially if my intention all along has been to piss away my career.

I don't really want that, though, do I?

No.

I just need some help in getting back on track.

But where would I find something like that?

Ah, fuck it.

"So what do you say, Benny?" I ask, back to focusing on the party. "You in?"

He stretches, covering his dick with the pillow I threw at him. I make a mental note to have all my furniture *and* their decorative accents, especially the pillows, steam cleaned.

Running his hand through his shaggy, dark blond hair, he says, "Am I in for what?"

"Party tonight," Nolan interjects in his usual no-nonsense tone. "One last blowout, and then Brent here says we're stopping with the bad behavior."

I have to laugh. Nolan is only three years older than me, but it's like he's twenty-five going on forty. He's the voice of reason in our crew.

Well, most of the time.

Not today, though. No, today he agrees to go all-out.

With the party plans full steam ahead, we get on our phones, texting and calling everyone we know.

"Tonight we party hard," I declare when we reconvene in the living room.

"Yeah," Nolan says, holding up a freshly opened bottle of beer.

"You mean hell, yeah," Benny corrects, raising the full shot glass in his hand.

"Hell, yeah," I echo, a beer *and* a shot on the table in front of me. "And just so we're clear," I add. "Tomorrow we give up the booze and the women. Tomorrow we start training for real."

The boys agree, and we drink to our plan.

Yeah, tomorrow we'll do all those things…

Read the rest of *Destiny on Ice* now:
Amazon: http://amzn.to/2gL1XC9